Down T

by

Kate Rigby

Acknowledgements

Heartfelt thanks to all those family members and friends who have supported me in my creative endeavours and to all those people I worked with in Bournemouth in the late 1980s and early 1990s in the addictions field.

for all those struggling with addiction

ADDICTION

1

Cheryl's all points and angles. You can see it in the crisp cut of her red lapel, the black cube of her heel, the sharp corners of her handbag, shining like rain. She splashed out on the suit especially for the interview and now she waits for her Surrey-bound train to rock her home. She pulls a couple of hairgrips from her tight bun, lets it unwind. But *drugs*. What was she thinking? It's hardly what you'd call a glamorous job, but when you haven't worked for years you have to take what's going. She smiles the thorny smile. Glorified secretary she'd call it, no matter how they dressed it up with the Team Assistant name.

The doors slam, the train lurches. It's getting too dark to see out unless she presses her face up close to the window, beneath the No Smoking sign, and sees beyond her faded lipstick. But if she lets her head roll back in her seat she can only see the dim reflections of other passengers. Over on the other side of the train is a mother with a little boy sleeping up against her. They've got a table on their side, with half a mushy biscuit on it. That's just what Michael would have done as a boy, sucked at some of his biscuit and then just left it there. Michael will be twenty now, wherever he is.

One day Michael might turn up and surprise her. In a suit or something. Nah, she can't ever imagine him in a suit. She can't see him in anything but the vague mid-teen clothes she last saw him in, his body thin and stooping, hunched in a chair like a shell. But she won't dwell on that, she must not.

She looks further down the carriage at the businessmen and women in their suits. She wants some of what they're having. She wants to feel zonked after a hard day's work, to fall asleep on her hand or keel over sideways into the aisles or pull out files on tables or fold her newspaper into four so she can attempt a couple of crossword clues and look like an executive.

The train bellows as it speeds along, and she turns her mind to the interview at the drugs project. It was in an old narrow building, that 484 place – both the name of the centre and the number of the road. The interviews were running late so she sat in the waiting area pretending to read a magazine.

"Nicola Stack? " the secretary called.

A pretty girl with bottle-blond hair and a leather jacket – some neolithic stones painted on the back - went to the desk. "It's *Nicky*. Got my wee in here." Nicky unzipped pockets inside her jacket and pulled out a specimen jar, full of golden liquid. "Here it is. It's been warming me baccy and chewie."

The secretary looked unimpressed. "You'll have to do another one, here on the premises."

"What's wrong with this then?"

"It's standard procedure. People have been known to bring in someone else's specimen."

"That's taking the fuckin' piss." Nicky seemed wholly unaware of her double entendre. "I can't pee to order."

Another member of staff with a more conciliatory tone offered Nicky a drink of water and escorted her off to a private cubicle. Without Nicky's protests to mask it, the sounds of a gruff male voice could be heard leaking through flimsy walls – something about *cooking it up.* Cooking what up? Cheryl stared through pages of mouth-watering recipes. He must mean *drugs.* Her thoughts spun. Shit, am I really cut out for this caper, even if it is only office work? Drug addicts are a frightening, aggressive bunch, aren't they? They're weak people too and she isn't very tolerant of human weakness. She was seriously thinking of walking out but then they called her in for her interview.

In fact, the interview panel looked favourably on her Life Experience and rusty secretarial experience. They seemed confident in her ability to Refresh Existing Skills and learn new ones: database, computer, statistics, and any other opportunities that might arise.

It's over four years since she last lived in London, south of the river. That's why she stood outside Camden Town tube, before her interview, waving her photocopied map at passers-by who said, Sorry, I'm only a visitor too, or Sorry, I speak not much English. That's the moment she might have turned back, because she felt this little shiver. Not just the December wind, but the draughty space all around her where family have always been, crowding her out. Family, kids, clutter.

Kids. How do they come about anyway? By default, usually. It was Andrew who wanted them in the first place, wasn't it? Or, rather, he didn't not want them. Children are the next progression after your wedding, aren't they?

It was Diana, her nextdoor neighbour in Tooting, who started her on this whole baby thing. She can still picture Diana's baby, fresh from hospital, its miniature fingers curling round her own tentative trunk of finger. Fingers so cold. "I thought babies were meant to be piping hot," Cheryl said, and Diana parcelled up the baby Viola and handed her over. "You better get some practise in, Cheryl. It'll be your turn next."

"Oh blimey, I wouldn't be seen dead up the spout, me." Besides, she didn't have the knack of holding babies. This one was wriggling about with all her tiny might, howling her head off.

Terrified she was too, that first time she had to babysit Viola. She couldn't settle to Diana's television with its different picture and knobs. Or to that slightly skewed view from the window – streetlamp and silver birch all shunted to the left, or to that uninspiring decor, all plain and muted. Then there were the pictures on the wall painted by Diana's husband, Iain. The bookshelves stuffed with textbooks and files and paperbacks by unknown authors. Well, she hadn't heard of them, anyway. She preferred her own bright house, all new and spirally with its modern lights and electric rings and snazzy wallpaper. Its blue hatch. Even Andrew's gun hanging over the grey-brick fireplace looked more homely. It was only an ornament, that gun. Because Andrew was a gentle, nervous sort who blinked a lot and hummed tunes to cover silences.

Where was all Diana's ruby nail polish, the spidery eyelashes in their plastic boxes, the 15 denier nylons that your nails sometimes snagged as you bunched them together for each partying foot? Diana didn't know anything about the bitter after-taste of Silvikrin hairspray on her way out to singing bluesy songs at the club with Peter de Cruz. Diana was a bit strange with her college ideas and loopy stare and enormous feet. That journal said it all. Cheryl fell upon it accidentally, creeping about the house as you do when you're babysitting, trying not to disturb the baby, thinking of things to do. She opened that diary with the sticker on the front saying 'Viola's Book' and started reading.

Iain planted the seed. I imagine the slow swelling, like apples plumping on the branch, round and luscious. The full-term dome of my belly. Firm, bronzed, fat as a pumpkin.

Now I'm always unalone. There is someone with me. We are one but two.

And then came those three immortal words – It's a girl. A beautiful daughter! I knew it. Womb of my womb. So big inside and so very tiny out here on my chest. Face all crinkled and stained with plum juice and little mouth all bubbles and gum or open-wide in a quivered cry. All wrapped up and snug in mounds of violet-white blanket with only her purple womb-moist head visible. And she's all mine! A beautiful girl, what else? We're floating off like an island, Viola and I. There's a pink mist all around us and I don't even hear Iain half the time.

Skylight eyes open up wide on the world each day like flowers. Viola. Named after your great grandmother, your maternal one. Then came mum, then me - now you. Together we're sowing the divine seed from age to age.

Just you and me, Viola. Us. We. Please don't interrupt us Iain with boring work talk because there's nothing more exciting and creative as the craft of motherhood. We rock together. When I rock, you rock. We have our own words. And if you fall ill, Mummy will take care of you. She'll take care of your nasty coughs and splutters because Mummy is magic. All mummies are magic. Mummies will come with cloths to wipe your face. Mummies will tuck in blankets and provide sweet blobs of milk for you to suck out with those little snorty noises. You gurgle. Pleasurable gurgles. You cry. Oh-so-pitiful cries. There there my petal, is it cuddles you want? I know, I know. It's nasty isn't it, being horizontal and alone and cooped up in darkness, even if it is a nice cradle that rocks. But it's not the same, is it? Not the same as company. Iain and I wouldn't sleep alone, would we? Though we're fully grown we still need each other and yet we expect you, a tiny baby, to sleep alone. Well, we'll make a space right between us, Daddy and I. A space for you in our bed. And by day I'll carry you upright in your new baby-sling where you can hold your sleepy sticky-thatch head against this side of my body-wall and listen to those now-faint sounds coming from the other side. Familiar sounds that soothe you ...

Cheryl thought it all peculiar. She couldn't ever imagine feeling like that about a baby, and then Viola started to cry. Cheryl shut the journal and froze. She thought babies slept once they were down. She peeped in and tried to make nice gurgly noises but it made matters worse, so she scooped Viola from the cot and carried her slowly down one stair at a time. Not continuous walking, but bringing her feet together on each stair before progressing on to the next, the way small children do, and it was just as well Diana returned when she did because Cheryl didn't have a clue how to decode the different cries of Viola.

The train slows as it approaches her stop. As she leaves the train station and heads back to her new home, she's glad she made the break. She's glad to have been refurbished and assumed her stage name: Cheryl West. Now, she's Cheryl the woman, not Cheryl the mother and drudge.

Her new Surrey home, Tea Rose Cottage, is not actually a cottage at all, but a pebble-dash dormer bungalow with the upper window peeping out from red tiles, like an eye from her past, keeping watch. It's set back from the other bungalows, well-hidden from the road, and reached by a long, straight drive, flanked by sculptured hedges and various stone animals, some decorative, some functional like the three penguins collecting rainwater in the bird bath on their heads. Not that she can see them properly in the winter dark, except those picked out by the garden lights. It's not really her style of place at all, but it belongs to a friend of Diana's, a dentist's widow who's gone off travelling to India for a year or two with Diana. The name of Tea Rose Cottage is carved into the oval of polished wood just to the right of the porchway where, in the glare of the security light, she catches sight of a figure huddled on the doorstep.

"Christ, Elaine, you nearly gave me a fright! What the hell are you doing here anyway?"

"Oh that's nice, that is...I've been freezing my butt off out here."

Elaine is full of the row she's had with some boyfriend or other.

Cheryl's heart drops as she unlocks the door and switches on lights. She really isn't ready to have her old life coinciding with the new.

"Smart suit that, mum. Where d'you get to anyway?"

"Job interview."

Cheryl puts her feet up and lights a cigarette.

"Did you get it?"

Cheryl shrugs. "I think so."

"When d'you start then?"

"It'll be after Christmas if I get it."

"Can I bum one off you, mum? Just smoked my last."

Elaine helps herself anyway, slides the ashtray over and perpetually taps her ash-free cigarette.

"Hey mum, when I was on the train I saw this bloke. Looked just like Michael. Well, from the back. I was willing him to turn round, then I got up and went to the loo so I could get a better look, and of course it wasn't him, was it? Do you ever do that?"

"What?"

"See Michael in everyone."

"Sometimes," she says, though she doesn't want to linger too long on Michael: where he is, whether he's come to any harm after so long with no word. You hear about bodies turning up years later, so badly decomposed that identification is well-nigh impossible. You hear about people assuming new identities. You hear all sorts. She supposes that Michael makes her feel – not guilt exactly – but some sense of failure. As a mother. That's why she's now Cheryl, the woman.

And then there was that time Andrew-

There was another woman, he said-

She blinks it away.

"Mum, can I stay here the weekend?" Elaine holds back her mousy hair into a ponytail, before letting it drop again. "*Please*. I've brought all I need."

"Go on then."

But Cheryl feels uncomfortable as Elaine pulls tufts in the fluffy animal doorstops, or rattles her nail file down the Venetian blinds, or pulls faces at the pictures of twee kittens and Home Sweet Home tapestries, left by the dentist's widow.

It wasn't always like this. She got pregnant at twenty-one, the age Elaine is now, and it gave her a big kick, as it did Diana. Those first few kicks blew her mind. "Quick Diana," she would say. "He's doing it again."

But it was a girl. All through her pregnancy she'd sworn blind it was a boy, but it was Elaine, and that was an even bigger miracle. She remembered Diana's words, womb of my womb, and she sort of knew what she meant. It was like a miniature version of yourself who could also have a miniature version of herself one day, and so on and so on. Like Russian dolls.

All wrapped up in a pink mist of bubbles and sticky hair, just as Diana had written. Lying in her good-as-new cradle, given by Diana. Soft as fondant and good enough to eat.

All hers to rock and dab and die for.

Oh what a buzz! She felt like a rock star, the most popular person on earth, like royalty. Cards piled in from everywhere offering congratulations, because everyone loves a baby, especially a new one, especially a first one, and people came to bill-and-coo and hand over little matinée jackets threaded with pink ribbon. And bonnets. And bootees. Especially for Baby. Elaine was like the baby Jesus, or something. Everyone's baby. The community's baby. The most photographed baby. People reached into the pram for just a stroke, just a tickle of baby cheek or finger, and she never thought it could happen to her but she was hooked on Diana's pink mist...

Then came Michael. Her longed-for boy. But he turned out to be his daddy's boy.

Then came Stephen. He was hers.

And fourteen years later – with her new lover – along came Juliet.

2

Dodo puts his foot down now they're on the motorway. He'd rather be driving a car as old as himself. A Triumph Herald or Hillman Minx or Vauxhall Cresta – each with its distinct grille and rear lights like tears or frowns or exclamation marks, or so he'd thought as a small boy. Instead he's driving a rusty black heap of Datsun, which isn't even his. He borrowed it off Judd. Well, Judd doesn't use the Datsun hardly – Judd drives that tinpot Ford most of the time.

Dodo loves driving. Loves reckless speed and danger and going beyond limits. Without getting caught. He never bothered with a driving test, though he's been able to drive since the age of twelve or thirteen.

"Stop at the next services." Nicky belches. "I'm gonna phone Judd."

It's already dark. Dodo remembers services by night. Looming like great ships with red and yellow lights right across the carriageway, and they'd get all excited in the back of the car at the thought of a fish and chip stop on their way to or from a seaside holiday. And then there was daytime on the motorway when his brother and sister quarrelled or played while he let his eyes track the lines of pylons and wires and poles as they dipped and rose. By the window. Always by the window. He only remembers bits, islands, because his memory isn't what it was. It's dark like a loft and he's scared to go up there.

"Getting out, Dodo?"

"Yeah. Need to stretch my legs."

"You look spaced out."

"All them lights. Red ones in front, white ones on the other side."

"Want something to eat?"

"Get us a veggie burger if we've got enough." He digs deep into his pockets. "Here's thirty pence more."

Nicky isn't his girlfriend, not really, though he's known her two or three years. They met on the streets, both runaway Londoners who knew the streets weren't paved with gold. They were fated to stick together from the start, him and Nicky. They've queued for soup and giros. They've shared doorways and sleeping-bags and Stonehenge, but they haven't shared much of their pasts. That's what he likes about Nicky, she never asks him personal questions and now he lives in the happy adult land of evasion and half-truths.

He knows all he needs to know about Nicky. She ran away from her last foster parents, she just couldn't hack it any more she said so she left. In true style. She made off with a china cat, one of a pair, made out of that thin, expensive china. She called it Sasha, and they used to take Sasha wherever they went – friend's floor, tent, back of a van – before Sasha had her accident which Nicky doesn't know about.

They've been camping in the middle of nowhere, him and Nicky.

"Did you know we were in the Cotswolds, Dodo?" Nicky said, coming back from the village store on that first morning, while he got into acid-mode so that he could hear the colour of the trees and smell their vapours, so that he could see the silver-birch lung when he looked in the lake. And when the acid was gone, Nicky still had her smack and they both had a bit of dope, which they smoked round the edges of the day to eke it out a bit longer. Man, I'm in orbit, Nicky would say, her eyes stinging and smarting from the evening campfire.

They coasted along, snuggling up together like winter nights, though it never goes any further. It's the heroin in Nicky's case. Takes away her need for sex and that's fine by him.

By day, they stomped on the ground and brought up the worms, they collected firewood, and got out the camping stove. This is the life, he thought. No one chasing them, just the wind fanning their hair: his dark brown ponytail, her blond hair, long enough to tie back now, only she doesn't.

Coasting along.

Until he saw the grains of fried rice on the stove jumping about like the maggots used to in his father's fishing box. Ugh.

Until he saw two fat tailor-made fags hanging like chalk from Nicky's mouth and knew they were running out of stores. She lit them both. Handed one across. "We've ran out of baccy and skins. And wacky baccy. We've ran out of everything."

No silver-birch lung, but his unshaved stubble in the rear-view mirror. "We've gotta get back, Dodo. There's not enough here for a proper hit and I've gotta get my script."

He doesn't care for the smack like she does. Once he's back in the Smoke, he'll revert to the fast stuff because it makes him feel real and alive.

He looks up. Sees her returning with one square of styrofoam.

"Got through to Judd," she says, as they sit on the bonnet, sharing the veggie burger.

"Yeah?"

"Yeah. Says we can share his new flat. Told you something would turn up, didn't I?"

3

Travelling to and from her now not-so-new job at 484, Cheryl finds she's glad to be a part of London again. Things may come and go in the provinces but in London things stay reassuringly unchanged: Les Miserables, Cats, The Tate and, as the weather improves, she has this urge to snatch a clump of cherry blossom as she crosses the city. Something to remind her of out there once she's cooped up inside the clammy 484 building – in the computer room, what's worse. More swearing goes on in that room than anywhere else in the building, except for the consultant's room where clients (as they're referred to at 484) flip if their scripts are unexpectedly reduced. Then you'll hear a blast of angry expletives, the reverberations travelling up even as far as the computer room. Mind you, this sort of thing happens surprisingly rarely from what she can gather, though she gathers very little up here on the fourth floor except for high-rise and low-rise histograms and bar charts and pie charts and tables. She gathers hoards of these, for Vernon, her supervisor: a little serious man with gold-rimmed glasses. No one envies her this job either. Statistics is one of those words that makes everyone scream and run a mile. Just lately she's had to stay late – later than her colleagues – to get her print-outs in a presentable form for some report or other that Vernon's preparing. Still here, Cheryl? they'll say, as one by one they leave the building. See you tomorrow then, Cheryl, I'm off on a home visit. Of course, Vernon's always around in the building at that hour, as is Mrs Jenkins the cleaner. If Mrs Jenkins gets as far as polishing the fire doors then Cheryl knows it's getting really late. She can't tear herself away from the computer and it's giving her all these headaches that become fully-fledged once she emerges into the dazzle of the streets.

Still, she prides herself on working hard and she's used to the heart-attack pace of London again, she's remembered how to move with it. On the tubes she remembers how the city wheezes and rattles over your head, and on the overground she's reminded of the number and the size of the tower blocks. Who lives in that one, fifteenth row up, fourth along from the left? Michael could for all she knows. He could be anywhere since none of them have seen him for nearly five years. He disappeared at the age of sixteen, the year before she started her new life in Bournemouth with Luigi and the baby Juliet.

Then again Michael always was a funny kid, wasn't he?

Well, no, not always, not at the beginning...

Today, like every other day, all she wants to do after work is flop into her home, Home Sweet Home, kick off her shoes and feel her feet expand. Why, she considers herself lucky if she has enough energy to add a few stitches to her tapestry at the end of each working day. Who'd have thought it: her and tapestry? It makes her feel her forty-something years. It's not her bag at all, it's just that there happened to be a few of them lying around, half-completed by the dentist's widow, so she thought, well, why not? It's got a certain compulsion about it. The one she's doing at the moment is really coming along. The reverse side is getting cluttered and she's finding it harder and harder to find somewhere for her finished-off threads. It makes her think of junkies and overworked veins and then she feels queasy.

But when she works on the front of the tapestry, it helps her unwind, and sometimes old memories creep in from long ago. As though she's trying to weave them in somewhere, into the bigger picture.

Michael was quiet when she carried him, not like Elaine with her great football kicks, but she was thrilled to bits when he was born. He was her longed-for boy, and she used to rock him boatwise in the cradle as he sailed off to sleep. We will rock you, rock you, rock you. By day, he would lie wriggling on his mat while she attended his every need, and she would hold him aloft, his eyes still a bright blue then, not the brown they would become, and watch his little alfresco tongue which she hoped would say reams, in time. Yes, the words would come, crudely at first, wonky, until he could chat and share things, like other little boys did with their mothers. He was going to be her very special boy ...

But he was his daddy's boy. And quiet like his father, though less so when the pair of them were together ...

*

Work soon becomes one big headache. It isn't only the VDU's, it's the artificial lights with their imperceptible flickers, it's the deafening printer that's always jamming and wrecking her tables and histograms. Even the shredder is now just another noise. When she first discovered it she thought it one of the seven wonders of the world; one of life's compulsive distracters like her tapestry, like popping bubble-wrap. It was so satisfying, that feeling, as her wads of ruined graphs were tugged into the serrated throat of the shredder and immediately minced to ribbons. But all the mechanical novelties have worn off because she doesn't want to work with machines all day, she wants to work with people and hear their words. If there was a team of them doing the graphs and things, and she their team leader, now that would be right up her street.

She decides to broach the matter with Vernon one day.

"You have to tell it to him straight," said Gina, one of the drug workers with a frizzy bob and bright asymmetrical earrings made of coloured plastic. "Otherwise he'll just think you're toddling along quite happily."

Gina's right, of course, and when Cheryl tells him of her aspirations, Vernon takes off his glasses and gives her a bewildered sort of look. "Oh I see. Well, in that case, I've got just the job. You can interview some of the clients for a survey about the services we provide, if I can just go through some of the methodology with you."

It wasn't quite what she had in mind. She's going to have to meet some real hardcore drug users. In years to come she has a feeling she'll always remember her first client, like drug addicts remember their first hit, it is said, and teenagers their first kiss, and mothers their first birth.

"I've found someone for you to practise on," says Vernon, the following week. "Someone to break you in gently. Someone helpful and friendly, with lots to say about the needs of drug users. Her name's Lesley Sweet."

*

Lesley turns up at her appointed time, something quite unusual according to staff folklore, which says you're lucky if they show up at all. It's especially unusual because Lesley's never met Cheryl before and there's nothing in it for Lesley – no script or counselling or favourable court report, no influential phone call. They're used to trading favours, she's heard. They live by deals. But Lesley's being truly altruistic on the face of it – she just likes to be of some help. Even so, Cheryl feels nervous at the prospect.

When Vernon introduces Lesley to her, Lesley stands up, holds out her hand and says, "How do you do?" Cheryl was expecting somebody more ill-mannered and unkempt. But in one fell swoop Lesley overturns most of the stereotypes. She's a nicely-spoken single mother in a smart peach two-piece, curly blond hair stacked up with combs and grips, her eyes wide blue innocents.

"It's good that someone wants to hear our views," says Lesley. "It's self-medication with me – it is with lots of us." And she lights her cigarette just like Cheryl, with elegance, as if it's an aesthetic healthy thing.

It all started, says Lesley, when her dad died. She was really gutted, because they were really close – she was a real daddy's girl. Anyway, this guy at this club where she used to work said he could get her something to take the pain away and it did for a while. Everyone was taking something, all her mates dabbled, you know, but she got into the heavy stuff in a big way. She soon lost all her friends, one by one. She was taking everything and anything. You name it. Then she slowly got it together. She did a detox, she saw counsellors, she had cognitive therapy. Anyway, she got back on her feet eventually and landed herself this super job showing tourists round Highgate Cemetery, but the responsibility made her nervous, so she started taking the gear again. She thought it would help her cope but it didn't so she left the job and went rapidly downhill again until four years ago when she had her little boy. Since then she's been a lot better. She hasn't had any gear for two months and she's down to 20 mls of methadone. She'd really liked to be stabilized on this amount, it's really difficult to come off methadone completely – much harder than heroin. She splits her methadone and takes half in the morning and half in the evening. Her mum used to have to dish it out to her, so she wouldn't drink a whole week's script in two days but she's able to take charge of it herself now.

"Occasionally, I buy a bit extra on the street, just in case, just for emergencies, you know," says Lesley. "It helps to know it's there. It's a bit of a psychological crutch, I suppose." She pauses to draw air. "Oh dear, I seem to have strayed right off the point, don't I? You'll have to tell me to shut up if I'm going on a bit. Oh yes, anyway, I think the services here are good. Everyone's always so nice and helpful. Suggestions for improvement? Let me think... "

It seems so bizarre, all of a sudden, sitting here discussing life on the edges with this very normal-seeming girl, who it's difficult to picture in some squalid loo somewhere, digging away at her arm, but, as Gina says, most of them haven't got two heads, most of them look just like you or I.

"Ah, here we are, I knew it was in here somewhere," says Lesley, handing something over from her handbag for Cheryl to look at. "A picture of my little boy. Taken at Southend."

Cheryl sees the little boy who looks a lot like Stephen did at the same age.

*

Stephen came along when Elaine was three and Michael two, and mother and baby bloomed in a sea of blue cards.

As a newborn he was at his best: crinkled, lip-quivering, still womb-fragrant, still a bit extraterrestrial. At a few days old, a few weeks old, he was just as riveting while he still had bubbles at his mouth and piercing eyes and closed fists...

But he was tinged with time. It seeped from him like a slow haemorrhage. She wished she could mop it up and keep him at that age for always, with people in supermarkets turning their heads for another look at his rare smallness. But it was a last look. You can't preserve it. It disappears. Then all you've got are your photos. Your photos and your memories. She remembers him sucking on his bottle, not her breast, but he was her baby and they were her breasts and he wouldn't suffer, not her bouncing baby. He would stand tall one day in a boy's world, where he'd have to let go of her hand and he wouldn't be able to cry or hug for many years and he'd only wash himself when told to and people wouldn't know what to buy him for birthdays or Christmas and he'd possibly consider a military career where he'd lose a leg or his mind or both and eventually become as bald as a coot.

But it was different being bald at this end of life, and he turned from purple to shrimp. He was just like a little bendy ball, God love him. Arms still pudgy, no juts. And the sounds he made were still without shape or form. Keep it that way, Stephen. Don't say a word. Just talk to me with your lovely blue eyes, because words bugger up the system. Listen to the way your brother and sister give me bloody earache in stereo, nagging me for sweets all the time.

But Stephen grew into a happy-natured toddler with a cheeky smile, and the lighter eyes of his father. He grew side by side with Josh, Diana's latest, and the two boys played and developed together. Their soft hair emerged from the same point on their twin crowns and they stood on wobbly bow legs, those same legs which felt robust when they clambered over their mothers. "It's all that testosterone," Diana said, still with all the scientific terminology at her fingertips from college days. "You should know, Cheryl – him being your second boy."

Cheryl glanced over at Michael, sitting quietly on the kitchen chair, engrossed in some colouring book, his feet not yet touching the floor. He was starting to be quite a sickly child, whereas Stephen was full of beans. Not only that, Michael didn't confide in her, didn't share things with her, like he seemed to with Andrew. His daddy's boy. And she turned to Stephen, balanced like a little monkey on her hip and gave him a kiss on his forehead where there weren't yet eyebrows, just little puckers. Stephen was hers.

*

A few days later, and Gina finds Cheryl someone else to interview for the 484 survey. "It'll have to be a home visit, though," says Gina, "and after work, because he's out during the day. But don't worry because he's okay. It's Jimmy Bird."

Cheryl's heard a lot about this Jimmy Bird. Gina says that there's probably a Jimmy Bird in every town. Jimmy Birds are in their late thirties or early forties and villains of the old school, whose code of conduct prohibits anything nasty like baseball bats or pit bulls or house burglaries. Jimmy Birds are friendly chatty sorts, liked by the drugs fraternity and drug agencies both. Jimmy Birds are family men with a couple of kids or stepkids in tow.

"I've always had a soft spot for Jimmy," says Gina, her frizzy mushroom-head tilted to one side. "Funny how you take to some more than others," and it makes Cheryl wonder whether people working with murderers and rapists have their favourites too.

But Cheryl discovers the accuracy of Gina's observations, as she sits on one of Jimmy's dog-clawed cane chairs in a house that smells of stale bacon. You can't help but like Jimmy, and there is, as expected, a little girl of five or six called Kelly and an older girl, Kathy, who is Jimmy's stepdaughter.

As the interview gets underway, Cheryl gives cautious glances at the open door because Vernon's drilled her about confidentiality, even when it comes to other family members. Especially with other family members. It's okay, says Jimmy, Kathy knows all about me and her old girl. Not that we do stuff in front of her. Nor Kelly. But Kathy's of an age where she knows what's what. Got an old head on young shoulders, know what I mean? Cheryl nods though she's bowled over by the ease in which he's opened up to a perfect stranger asking him personal questions in his own home. To be honest, Cheryl, he says, Kathy's at that age where she's embarrassed by us. Dead anti us. Never brings her mates home or nothing because she's embarrassed by our Van Morrison and Eric Clapton records and Anne's Indian capes. Would you credit it? It used to be the older generation what was worried about their kids getting mixed up in sex and drugs and rock 'n' roll, know what I mean? Have you got kids, Cheryl? (She flushes and says four). Four? You'll know what I'm on about then. You're about my sort of age. To be honest, I think Kathy'd be happier if we looked like a couple of boring old farts, he says, laughing raucously, and she still feels uneasy about the open door and decides to go to the toilet, shutting it on her return. It works for ten minutes perhaps, then Kelly bounces in and climbs on Jimmy's knee. Who's that lady, she asks in a loud whisper and Jimmy, almost eating her ear, says, She's a lady who's talking to daddy. Kelly then runs to get her latest painting, proudly showing it to Jimmy, describing all the elementary figures and objects and activities in it at great length.

Jimmy, like Lesley Sweet, then starts to go off at interesting tangents and gives graphic details about his life during the past twenty years. Most of it isn't relevant to the study but he wants to tell it anyway. He's a likeable crook, it's true, and one of a dying breed where honour-among-thieves still holds true – he'd only swindle insurance companies or the taxman or the Social Security, not private individuals. When he does get to the point, he says things which make her sit up. He says HIV is one of the best things that's happened as far as many addicts are concerned, because now people are thinking about what addicts want. And she wants to say, D'you really think so? Aren't they just thinking of themselves, worried that HIV might come their way, God forbid, if they don't contain it? But she bites her tongue. Whichever way you look at it, it's still a desperate thing to say – that you're glad of a killer virus. Jimmy says, Yeah, at last people are waking up to the fact that most of us don't want to stop doing drugs. I do drugs because I enjoy them and I know I'm speaking for the majority.

It's all still going round in her head as she leaves Jimmy's. Her neck hurts. That's where all the stress goes after such intense listening and writing. Straight to the muscles of her neck and gives her one of her headaches. Or maybe it was the surprise mention of her kids that did it.

It was that painting of Kelly's, that was it. Took her straight back to Elaine's first days at playschool. She remembers how some kids didn't even notice their mums quietly slipping out, while others bawled and bawled. Elaine was of the former camp. That was good, wasn't it? Better to be like that than all clingy, though a little weep from Elaine on her departure wouldn't have gone amiss. When she came to collect Elaine, she was greeted with sheets of damp paintings hanging from both her daughter's hands. Look mummy! Look what I drawed! And Cheryl felt reassured because there was that connection which Diana had written about in Viola's baby journal; that age-to-age thread right there in Elaine's picture: the narrow band of sky looking lost at the top of the page, the redundant expanse in the middle, the matchstick figures standing like trees, taller than the little house beside them.

For the most part, Elaine was still living in a world where child-trees have toes you mustn't step on and toothbrushes have curly hair, and Mondays are red, and Wednesdays green. At the stage of the ever-divisible why, as Diana called it.

– Why has that man got a newspaper over his face, mummy?

– Because of the sun.

– Why?

– I dunno. Because he doesn't want to get sunburnt.

– Why?

– Sunburn hurts, that's why.

Why why why.

Diana always said playschool was the start of the slippery slope. It chipped away at more of the Pink Haze, she said. The Pink Haze of birth and babyhood. One thing was certain, things did change once Elaine went to the Big School. Cheryl then became a mum with a different emphasis. She had to soothe Elaine's head after a bad day, and make jellies for her friends, and share her with teachers and dinner ladies and other children. She had to acquire a whole new set of 'friends' – the mothers of Elaine's best friends – who she had nothing else in common with.

Then Michael started playschool, and she was fast losing them. Soon it would be Stephen's turn and she clung desperately to his pushchair, but there really wasn't time to dwell on it. There were so many chores, punctuating her day. The laborious chants would accompany her as she rolled the pushchair along. *Loo roll cotton wool matches marg. Loo roll cotton wool matches marg.* On and on, these menial household raps. She would have most of the essentials written out on a list beforehand, but sometimes new or forgotten items would pop into her head en route to the shops. If she ever lost her list she was at her wit's end. My list Andrew, she would say. Have you seen it? And Andrew would look up at her, though he didn't seem to hear her. Andrew's was a very exact and ordered world, like his work in Air Traffic Control.

There were the odd frumpish signs creeping in too: the wind would catch her skirt, any old skirt these days, and a smile would break open her face when she remembered the passion-killer knickers she had on or the great potatoes at the top of her tights.

At home she would unpack her bags and hoover the house and play with Stephen, and wonder if there was more to life beyond this programme of buying cooking feeding cleaning, which would go on and on remorselessly until or unless she called a halt. Then, afraid of these unsettling thoughts she would return to the security of her list and begin ticking or crossing. Hee hee, I can cross something else off my list, she would say, and out loud, because in the short term it gave her a profound sense of satisfaction, this crossing out of things. It gave her the same transient thrill as filling up black sacks with empty milk cartons and old sprays and out-of-date fuel bills. But what if she ever reached the end of her list? What if there was only the great Void?

Come on, Cheryl, she would tell herself. You're letting yourself go. Get some of that glamour back. Call up Peter de Cruz at the club and start singing the blues again. Anything!

4

Dodo crawls out of bed, late afternoon.

He aches. He wheezes. He coughs. He rolls a cigarette. He staggers to the front room window for some air. On the other side of the street, there's a young girl of about twelve in a tight skirt, skateboarding backwards and forwards past that black kid who's out there with his ghetto-blaster. Dodo slams the window down. He doesn't like rap. He limps across to the kitchen, where his little black cat is licking the rim of one of the saucepans, piled high in the sink.

"Oi Merlin," he says, pouring some milk into a saucer. Merlin jumps down and heads straight for the milk, giving it one cautious lick. Then thirstily attacks it, splashing it everywhere.

This flat he and Nicky share with Judd is above a boarded-up old shop. You can still make out the lettering – Gibb's Ironmongers – if you look carefully. Judd says it's not a flat but a maisonette because it's on two floors, but when Dodo thinks of maisonettes he doesn't have in mind places like this. It's the kind of building where pigeons gather on the ledges high up and leave behind their white-and-black signatures on turrets and tiles. He feeds the pigeons from the top floor windows and there's a balcony outside one of them but it's not meant for standing on: it's just for decoration. If he could, Merlin would jump right out onto the balcony and frighten the hell out of the pigeons, but instead he's got to make do with a bird-show through glass, which makes his jaws judder.

The flat's a health hazard. When you turn on taps, all the damp lice and silverfish dart. When you switch on the lights, cockroaches scuttle off into shadows. There's fungus in the bathroom and people scratch their ankles and say there's fleas in the carpet.

The flat's a safety hazard. When you plug things in, sockets move and sparks appear. The whole structure is unstable and at the back of the house they're putting up scaffolding. Someone must think it's worth saving then, not like that row of ex-shops up the road, half-bulldozed.

Dodo sits on his bed, worn out. He never feels properly awake, only chemically. The wind rattles the windows. He pictures it as a thing you see, like smoke, as it curls through the gaps. Just the weather for our kites, his father used to say. He laces up his Doc Martens. He hears the street door slam and Nicky's heavy-duty boots on the bare wood stairs.

She dumps her leather jacket on the floor. "Where you off, Dodo?"

"The Spar."

"Get us some skins can you? And a Yorkie."

The Spar shop over the road stocks everything, but most stuff in there contains animal fats or gelatin. Not only that, but the Asian family who run it often hold his notes up to the light, before putting them in the till. But he puts up with it because he can't be arsed to walk the extra few hundred yards to the supermarket.

He wouldn't like to work in a shop. He wouldn't like to work anywhere, as it goes, which is just as well because he won't get a job now. Not in this state. Not that he cares. He's useless at timekeeping and dressing to suit. He once started some work experience in a factory when he was still at school. On his third morning there, he made it as far as the gates but he turned round again and never went back. It was the same when he used to dawdle to school, timing it so he'd arrive too late and so off he would go: lighter, relieved, the whole world in a classroom except him and not a kid over five in sight – only mothers with babies going about their morning shopping. And back home, if the house wasn't empty, his dad wouldn't make him go back to school, not if he didn't want to.

*

People come and shout up at their window for the keys to the street door and Nicky – it's usually Nicky who answers – slings them down. You can hear the jingly clank as they hit the pavement.

People stay for spur-of-the-moment parties, though they're the most dire parties ever. People like Annabel who's a real party animal; who needs to party every night, otherwise she feels she's missing out. She sticks on Jimi Hendrix and blasts out those 'young' telly addicts next door who bang on the walls and Dodo turns the music up even louder and calls them pillocks. They're just Philistines, says Annabel, with a toss of her long auburn hair. Her own record collection, her singles' one, spans from The Kinks to Soft Cell where it suddenly ends. There hasn't been anything worth buying after those fifteen years of musical brilliance, she says. But she approves of all his warped records – his Joni Mitchell and Doors and Procol Harum and T.Rex. She loves to sing along powerfully, from the heart, which reminds him of his mother singing the blues. You've got good taste, Dodo, Annabel says, even though you're too young to remember them. I've got memories to go with them. I've lived them.

She's a sixties person all right, with her small heroin habit and her huge pot one, which she pays for by dealing. She once told Judd that dealing makes her feel the centre of attention and activity, because everyone comes to her and it makes her feel dead important and powerful.

Then there's Freddie who comes round not to party, but to use the bath. Nicky once walked in on him by mistake and he was lying there starkers in the empty bath. He was well out of it she said and he was clicking his fingers – first one, then the other – all sort of slow and deliberate. Annabel didn't believe Nicky at first but she's now heard the clicking too, through the loo wall or outside the bathroom door. Sometimes, before using the bath, Freddie will say, dead serious, Got any soap? And Judd will say, Yeah, you can find it due east of the cockroaches and slightly west of the magic mushrooms sprouting out the grout. Judd can always think of clever answers like that and then there's that Tim bloke who everyone hates because he never shares his joints and does things that he thinks are funny, but no one else does, like shaking his cans of beer and fizzing them open over everyone and he calls Nicky an airhead and he used to talk about selling Sasha for half a grand before Sasha had her accident.

And then there's the electric-light-girl who had such a bad trip she never came back and now the lights are out to get her permanent – they plot and spark and pull nasty faces at her …

5

Gina gives Cheryl her third 'client': an Asian woman, known to all as Dixie. Dixie's okay if you get her on a good day, says Gina, but Cheryl makes the mistake of dipping into Dixie's file the day before they're due to meet. Just the thickness of the file itself – now battered and as thick as an encyclopaedia – is intimidating. Dixie's one of these people known to every agency: housing, social services, probation, police – each playing its part in this computerized tapestry of her life. To her name, Dixie has two broken marriages (both violent, and currently teamed up with Duke, a notorious dealer not to be messed with), three children (one of them on glue), four suicide attempts, an eating disorder, and a history of prostitution, drug dealing and spells in Holloway. It all seems to stem from the time when her lover was murdered when she was seventeen.

Cheryl feels the coils of tension in her body as she prepares to meet the awesome Dixie. On such a searing hot day, it doesn't feel right being in the city. She passes a group of boys playing football near the subway, breathing in nothing but car exhaust and the sight of them makes her pine for water without limits, for a place where every corner is licked by the sea. For Bournemouth.

She remembers how envious she was when Diana moved down from London to Bournemouth in the mid-seventies. "I'm coming to stay down there this summer, Diana," Cheryl told her. "Just try and stop me."

She pictures them all as they were that summer: she, Diana, and their five kids. She pictures the day she told Diana about this thing between her and Peter. Peter de Cruz.

"There's some wine in that carrier bag, Di. Fancy some?"

"It'll go right to my head in this heat."

"Oh go on."

"Just a drop then," said Diana, checking the whereabouts of her children. Viola, now twelve, was swimming in the sea, and Josh was helping to construct a large moated sandcastle in the harder sand along with Cheryl's three. "I don't want them to see me tight."

"You should worry!" Cheryl said. "Mine have all seen me the worse for drink. But then I'm beyond the pale." They laughed, and then Cheryl said, "So go on. How's life really in Bournemouth? How's things with you and Iain?"

"Well..." Diane sipped some of the wine from her plastic cup. "Well, you know how it is once the kids come along. We don't have much of a physical relationship any more. He's dog-tired when he gets in from work."

Cheryl pulled a knowing face as if to say, Tell me about it. "What you need, Di, is someone to spice up your life. "

"What, you mean have an affair? Oh no, I wouldn't go that far." Diana went quiet. She seemed deep in thought for a moment. And then she said, "You're not having an affair are you, Cheryl?"

Cheryl smiled. A confidential sort of smile. "Let's say Peter and I have always had a certain chemistry. Brushing up close on stage, a kiss on my neck, you know the sort of thing. Don't get me wrong, I've not been unfaithful, you know. But Andrew and me are like you and Iain. It's all work with him too."

"But I wouldn't really change any of it," said Diana. "And Iain's such a loving father."

"Oh they're all that, Di. In Andrew's spare time he takes Michael kite-flying or fishing because no one else in our house can be bothered with such boring hobbies. Stephen's more energetic. He likes proper boys' things. Look at him now. He's the one who runs and digs." She looked at her youngest with pride. "Not only that, he's very bright academically too. A real credit to me he is."

"So you've started up the singing again then?"

"Indeed, Di. Well, you've got to have something to look forward to after banging away at an old typewriter half the day."

Cheryl felt the passion rise in her voice when she spoke about Peter and the songs. We sing Billie Holiday, she said, and some of Peter's songs, just like old times, and I drink snowballs or shorts with a cocktail stick and a cherry on the end, which Peter feeds into my mouth. He's so suave, Di. He once popped the question, you know, but I married Andrew because Andrew's dependable. Anyway, Peter seemed too old at the time. When I was nineteen he was over twice my age. He was also too dominant, that sort of man will control you, and no man will ever control me, and without warning she was telling Diana about this man, this friend of her father's, who always used to pay her compliments when she was still at school. He arranged to give her singing lessons and train her voice, this man, until one day, the worse for drink, he tried to force himself on her and she had to give up the singing lessons after that.

She was suddenly sorry that she'd said so much to Diana. It was the drink or the sun or the combination, and she found a quick escape route in a scene brewing up between Michael and Stephen.

32

"Michael's taken my flags, mummy."

She looked at Michael with belligerence. "Did you take them? Well, did you?"

He shook his head but she knew he was lying which made her want to swipe him. "And I don't like horrid little boys who tell lies either. Now give them back to Stephen at once!"

She turned to Diana. "They're getting grumpy. It's probably time I rounded them up. Hand us the towel, Elaine."

Elaine was enrobed in the huge bath towel and trying to slip off her damp bikini inside her self-made tent. "I'm trying to get dressed."

"Oh come on," Cheryl sniggered. "You're nine years old, for God's sake. It's not as if you've got anything to hide yet."

*

Dixie lives on a run-down council estate, which, according to Gina, is full of people avoiding TV detector vans and bailiffs and loan sharks and rival dealers.

When she gets to number 48, Cheryl tries to make her knock sound friendly and non-authoritative. There's no reply for ages, but eventually a voice from inside shouts *Who is it?* Cheryl reminds Dixie of their appointment and there's much unlocking of bolts and security chains before Dixie – her face not without charm in spite of the scarring – peers round the door. Sorry, says Dixie, but I don't usually answer to folk who don't use the special code. Five short rings.

While Dixie makes drinks, Cheryl thinks of the daunting file and Duke and the violent partners and the child on glue and the murdered lover, and she puts on her toughest face. But once Dixie sits down with her coffee in front of her, she becomes fluid and vibrant. Her every gesture says something, like the way she stirs her coffee with her heavily-bangled wrist. Even the little baby in the little cradle-seat is darker and prettier and more exotically named than Juliet.

Juliet – her darker baby, late in life, with Luigi ...

You lot only see the tip of the iceberg, says Dixie through the curls of smoke, billowing dragon-like from her nostrils, and Cheryl avoids the gaze of the pretty baby in the cradle-seat.

It's only the tip, I'm telling you, Dixie goes on, because there's millions of speed freaks won't go near your 484. Nothing down for them. Not that I understand the mentality of people who do speed. If you're going to do it, do it properly, yeah? Coke is the real thing, sweetie. Who needs speed in London anyhow? You get it in the tubes and in the shops and in the pubs and in the clubs, yeah? There's always that buzz. Always a beat, yeah? Everyone and everything moves except the fucking traffic, she says and neighs like a horse, which exposes her large, striking gums. She touches Cheryl on the arm. Tell you what though, babe, if you're going to open a place for the speedies you should have it on the top floor and call it the Upper Storey, yeah?

As Cheryl emerges into the heat, her head goes round and round with it all. Dixie is right about the traffic. The bikes are the only form of transport making any headway through lines and lines of crawling cars, and she thinks about the exotic baby who looked not unlike Juliet at that age, before she was lost to words and the black hole of time.

*

At 484, they use the word non-judgemental a lot. It's one of those words they're all trained to use and constantly aware of. It means not looking down on, or up to their 'clients' not patronizing them. Just meeting them eye to eye. On the level.

Except the staff at 484 can be completely judgemental when they want, Cheryl especially, though it's tongue in cheek and behind the scenes. They all need this sort of humour to lighten their days. Like the other day when Cheryl suggested to Gina that Dixie switch to bottle-feeding because as it stood the poor little bugger was probably being fed pure methadone. And Gina said that Alice Astor was as straight as a zigzag.

This last bit of information was important for Cheryl to know, Gina said, since Alice was next on Cheryl's list, her hit-list, as Gina called it.

The rest of the Drug Team agree that Alice is the arch manipulator with her little whining voice which begs so pathetically, Can you phone Housing Benefits for me? Can you give me a lift as far as– ? Can you get Dr Sharma to give me some more Temazepam? Alice has got that tearful choke to a tee, she's got them – pharmacists, doctors, probation officers, each and every one – jumping through hoops to help her. But don't be conned, says Gina, behind that display of complete helplessness is one artful lady. Oh don't worry, says Cheryl, no one can pull the wool over my eyes.

But it's Alice's mother Cheryl ends up drinking tea with from a bone china cup, rattling nervously on the saucer as together they survey the quiet greenness of the garden and canal, near Camden Lock.

Mrs Astor is a demure little woman, scrupulously polite, and very apologetic about her daughter's absence. What can I say, says Mrs Astor. This is typical. This sort of thing happens all the time. They forget things, you see. You can't trust them with important information. It's the same with money. Alice went through all her grandfather's inheritance in a matter of weeks. We didn't even know she had a problem back then, Charles and I. Of course, in our will we've arranged for Alice's share to be put in trust. It's been terrible, it really has. Alice sold lots of my jewellery including my mother's wedding ring, you know. She's only twenty-two but sometimes she seems so old, older than us. Mind you, at other times she's just like a child, a lost little girl. We persuaded her to come back here to live, you see. That way we can at least keep an eye on her and know what she's up to, but it restricts us. We can't leave her. One of us has to be here virtually all the time because if our backs are turned for one moment, she'll try and sell something – like the video or CD player. There was that time when we returned from the Chelsea Flower Show and found the spare television set gone. None of us are getting any younger and Charles isn't too well. She used to be such a sweet-natured thing too. We still get glimpses of our little Alice, but they're becoming fewer and further between. It's a bit like Jekyll and Hyde. Would you like to see a photograph? Here she is. This was taken when she was in the sixth form. She did really well in her A Levels, you know. She was such an attractive girl. She still could be. But all the young girls have these untidy hairstyles these days, don't they?

Do you have children, Cheryl?

You have to be there for them, don't you?

Yes, she can see Mrs Astor has been there for Alice. You wouldn't have caught Mrs Astor sleeping around with beach vendors while visiting her best friend in Bournemouth.

Oh, but it was worth it. Life had become insufferable in London. She was planning to separate from Andrew, even file for a divorce, (except she didn't want to go public with any of it). Michael had left home, and vanished into the ether. Elaine was a moody teenager, hardly ever home herself and Stephen was away at school during term-time, while her own singing nights had dropped off because she was drinking too much, Peter said, and it wouldn't do turning up to bookings late and drunk.

She could no longer stomach the housewife routine either: those simple, monotonous acts, like removing her rings and bracelets, ready to make a start on the washing-up, catching sight maybe, of a tea-stained jay-cloth, lying like a rotting fish on the draining board. Perhaps squeezing the slimy thing out and dunking it in a bucket of bleach with a whole lot of others, before scooping out another with a whole new lease of life.

Andrew would sometimes be hovering nearby, when he wasn't avoiding her, but she'd all but stopped talking to him. It was better that way, than to argue constantly. There was a little grey creeping into his brown hair, a few furrows here and there, and he was thickening out, as men do around forty, though she supposed he was still attractive. But she couldn't look at him objectively any more.

On one such occasion she just said it. "I can't go on like this. I'm taking a break. I'm going down to visit Diana for a couple of weeks in Bournemouth."

Mrs Astor is asking her about the physical effects of all these drugs on their brains. Some of them must get permanent brain damage, mustn't they? Alice just doesn't seem to remember things from one day to the next. Today is a case in point and muggins here is left with the embarrassing job of apologizing on her behalf. She wasn't brought up to forget her manners, you know. Then again, allowances have to be made because she's ill, isn't she? Do you meet others like her? We often wonder, Charles and I – why Alice? Often wonder where we went wrong, and Cheryl wants to say, but sometimes there's just no mileage in whys or wherefores. Maybe Alice was simply bored and just wanted a bit of excitement.

Cheryl likes to pretend that's all she was looking for down in Bournemouth, that hot summer. Not spite, not revenge, just good old-fashioned excitement. Nothing more. It was so refreshing, after London, to glimpse the cool, sparkly sea. There was a half-naked mass seething at its fringe, which you had to pick your way through before settling on your own square yard of sand. Then they came into focus, your beach neighbours for the day, and she and Diana would make fun of them all.

"Hey, Di, see that old man in the deckchair up on the prom with his head back, gob open? You got the one?"

"Well, don't look round, Cheryl, but there's a couple behind *welded* together in a kiss. Honestly."

"Say, *he's* a bit of a poseur.

"Hey, you don't think we're getting a bit long in the tooth for all this, do you, Cheryl?"

"Bollocks. I'm in my prime."

Choc ices, ice lollies! Choc ices, ice lollies!

The beach vendor always passed them, several times, going up and down the beach with his box of frozen treats. A dark-skinned bloke, sun-glasses propped on his forehead, and not bad-looking in spite of his slightly protruding teeth. About thirty-two, Cheryl would have said, which turned out to be spot on, she discovered later. "Can

I interest either of you ladies in a choc ice?" he said, though from the moment he sat on his ice-box, Cheryl knew she was the one he was after. He handed them both a little icy package. "Here, have these on me."

He asked them their names. He told them he was called Luigi.

Cheryl looked at him with mock disappointment. "Where's the Italian accent? It sounds pure Bournemouth to me."

He smiled and started doing exaggerated Italian gestures. "My mamma, she English. I broughta uppa over here."

Cheryl laughed, but she could sense Diana's annoyance, with both her and Luigi. "Look, I'll see you later, Cheryl. We're eating about seven, OK?"

And so Cheryl met Luigi again on the beach the next day, and the next.

She felt like a teenager again as they lay on their beach mats side by side, hands interlocking, and only parting to smear sun oil into each other's back. They were still there when the sands emptied out at tea-time, when the metal-detectors came, scouring the sands for the day's rich pickings, and then the office workers would come, hot-footing it from the office, to soak in the edge of the day.

They were like this too, she and Luigi. On the edge of things. They would watch the moon come up, and the sea curling round the wooden supports of two empty deckchairs, and they would each sit in one, dangling their toes in sea froth.

By day, they spent so much time in the water, paddling mostly, and Luigi would bring a four-pack of lager which he kept chilled by digging a hole at the water's edge, and the waves would wash their ankles too and cool their passion as they stood on the edge of things.

"I don't want to go home," she said. "What am I going to do when –?" He put a sealing finger on her lips. "Shh. Don't worry, Cheryl. Let's just enjoy what time we have together."

But her time was running out, she knew, as she made her way down to Bournemouth beach on that very hot day. She was due to go back home the following day. Go home and face her failing marriage. Their usual spot was overrun with children, wasps swaying around overflowing bins, and she felt hemmed in.

"I came here to get away from families, Luigi."

"Looks like the weather might break anyway", he said. "How about my place?"

Dare she? But she thought he'd never ask. This was life at its best. Pure spur-of-the-moment stuff. Other people were carrying on as normal in the sunless heat – washing sand from their toes under the taps along the prom or brushing it off the soles of their feet from parked cars. It got everywhere if you didn't – in the sheets, in the towels, and suddenly big no-nonsense raindrops fizzled out on the hot-plate ground. But they kept falling. Vertical, thundery, speckling the prom.

The rain brought out the foul smells from dustbins and refuse sacks, as they hurried back to Luigi's between cloudbursts and fits of laughter. The sky was black, the pavement covered in a dark sheen. They were drenched, but once indoors they dried each other with vast male-smelling towels.

Just the two of them rubbing each other's hair dry and removing each other's damp clothes and sipping hot coffee.

They drank all the coffee they needed and The Lotus Eaters played on the radio, First picture of you, first picture of summer, see the flowers scream their joy, and their thighs were hot and hungry. The meal always tastes good when you've had to wait a bit for it, Luigi said, and then they left their words in a heap on the floor with their wet clothes. Words were for stupid people who didn't have the art of real communication, words were for dressing in and hiding behind, for the self-conscious and the inhibited. Words weren't for them, not there, not then. Sounds yes. Grunts, sensual and primitive. Kisses, wet and tonguey.

But how quickly pleasures pass. They were already fumbling on the floor to pick up their words again – their soppy love-words. They couldn't stand to be undressed and silent for long, even while they caressed each other's dishevelled hair and drank more coffee and got hiccups. They couldn't function without their words when it came down to it. It was an illusion. They thought they'd caught it for a split second. Like the white trail of aeroplanes: clear for a moment, then dissolving in the sky without trace.

6

Dodo is woken by something. Not the black and white TV in his room, still on from last night, but the Pillocks next door. With their drill. He wants more sleep, though he's been here centuries. If he walks down to the front room, he might see people he's never met before. His kids' kids. But the Pillocks haven't gone, for sure, they're still hacking about with that fucking drill. He gropes for an object, something to bang on the wall with. He can't find anything hard enough. The bones in his fist will do and he strikes the wall. Bang bang bang. That should shut them up.

It doesn't. Blast them out with your music then. But the AIWA. You fucking sold it, didn't you? No point hanging on to it when most of your old 60s and 70s records and tapes have all been sold for a quick fix. That or nicked.

He turns over in bed. There's a squashed dog-end on his pillow. He must have fallen asleep with it. You're a fuckin' liability they're always saying. You're a fire risk, Dodo, d'you know that?

It was Nicky's idea to swap rooms, so she and her new dude, Stu, could have the big room together. Dodo didn't like that room, anyway. No proper curtains and the criss-cross scaffolding and builders looking in all the time. This room up here's a bit small and fishy, but it's got the balcony and the pigeons.

It's late in the afternoon. He can tell by the light and shadows. He gets up and limps down to the kitchen where the sun's streaming in. He struggles to lift the window a bit more but the sash cord's broken. On the sill outside, Nicky's put out new broken bread over those black fossils of crust, rained on for weeks.

He knows what his body needs.

Just a little speed and he'll be back on top.

*

Suddenly he's feeling scared. Something to do with the scaffolding pipes. The feet trudging across the planks between them. Heavy disconnected Drug Squad feet.

The world's getting ready to bite him.

He scurries to the bathroom where it's safer because there aren't any windows, but he forgot about the mirrors that multiply your reflection ten times over. Your unshaven look, reminding you of your father's five o'clock shadow. Better to have been a girl.

There's nothing new under the son –

 Did he shout out loud then?

Voices from the dark loft.

But where's the silver-lung and the crystal-heart? Scaffolding pipes point through the mirror and turn into a million rifles and he grabs at one which shatters into a kaleidoscope of eyes and he hears a static buzz in the walls like one of those ultraviolet machines that zaps flies and falls down a dark chute onto the blade which cuts his thoughts.

*

The smell of singeing blanket wakes him. He must have fallen asleep by the gas fire. Others were here before, rolled up in blankets, shining, shivering wet beads from their brows. Groaning. I'm fucking dying, man. But they've all gone, the smackheads. Left him to kip by the fire till he started singeing. Something's gone cold on him. Under him. Like a cold hot water bottle. Only soggier. A burst one then or a leaking one or knocked-over coffee or maybe he's pissed his pants like a stupid kid…no, it is a cup, he can feel the hard china in his rib and he thinks of the smashed Sasha and the pieces he swept up and dumped at the bottom of the wheelie bin so Nicky would never know. But it was an accident. You're always breaking things. He couldn't think where he was for a moment. His ear's pressed to the floor, the ear that hears the empty space below, the ironmonger space. The space that merged with his dreams.

There was a little girl in his dreams, seven years old. Her dad came to see her on an access visit but she wasn't happy. She was angry. She had power, that kid, standing on the inside looking out through shop doors that turned into French windows. There was a football at her feet and she gave it a good hard kick through the open French windows and up the lawn and said, Strength is distance.

He understands it now. Physical and mental distance. That age-old kid suddenly gave way to the boat with the collapsible table, like the one they took on the canal, him and his father…

He turns his back on –

He turns on his back –

Stares at the yellow ceiling and mentally doodles on it. Figures of eight and huge petals. Hears a Golden Earring song in his head.

No more speed I'm almost there
Gotta keep cool now gotta take care

Sees a dead spliff in the ashtray and smokes the rest of it down to the bone in his fingers.

He feels exhausted.

He needs buoying up and didn't he dream of his brother going back to his posh school after the summer holidays?

Strength is distance, he thinks and crashes out.

7

It can make your head spin sometimes, working in this field. Cheryl supposes this must be why so many people leave. She watches one of the outreach workers clearing his desk and ripping up things he won't be needing again. He's clearly one of those people who can just give up addictions work, cold turkey, while others seem to be addicted to this line of work and get a vicarious buzz from the lives of addicts. It's easy to get hooked, though she wouldn't quite include herself in this group. Nevertheless, she no longer fears them. Of course, there is the aggressive element, no doubt about it, but Gina says most of the addicts are sunken people, sunk into the depths of their addiction and generally happy to oblige, provided they get their full quota of methadone. The kind of people, she says, who have been flung out of life and all they want now is their one little luxury and to be left alone.

Gina, Vernon and the other workers may have a little moan today, but they'll be back for more tomorrow while Cheryl finds it a convenient working atmosphere; everyone's far too busy to get to know each other on a more intimate footing. Everyone, that is, except Marcia, one of the secretaries, who has more time for the personal, especially over lunch. Cheryl wonders, in fact, as she replaces the plastic cover over her computer whether she should start taking her lunch up in the office. Or trot off to a pub somewhere, because the lunch area downstairs is too small and airless and claustrophobic. It's the place where Marcia sits in her usual chair, wholemeal sandwiches and yoghurt on her lap, asking her personal questions. "What are you doing at the weekend, Cheryl?" she'll say, and Cheryl will shrug, and say, "Dunno yet."

Marcia is sticking to lunch-room protocol less and less, and today she says, "Is it your youngest son, Cheryl, who's at university?"

"Stephen? Oh yes. He's doing an Economics degree up in Manchester."

Marcia unclips her sandwiches from their plastic casing. "A bright boy, then."

Cheryl hovers near the magazine table, avoiding eye contact with Marcia. "Yes," she says. "He always was really clever. Lapped up the books, he did."

"And what about your other son? Is he a book worm too?"

"Not as much." Cheryl snatches hold of a magazine to end the conversation, but it's already unleashed a memory of when she was asked to go up to the school once, when Michael was seven or eight, to discuss his progress with his form teacher. Michael sat outside in the cloakroom, under the bare pegs, wheezing into his blazer, while she learned how far behind he was with his reading. "I know he's been absent a lot with his asthma," said his teacher. "That's why I was thinking that one hour's reading practise every night with you or his father would help him a lot."

And she did try. She took it on herself to be the one, but it was such hard work. She remembers one occasion when Andrew had taken the boys out for the afternoon to fly their kites. When they returned, she said, "Well, boys, did you have a good time?"

And it was always Stephen who answered. "We saw a rescue helicopter, mummy. We saw three of them flying low, didn't we, daddy?"

Behind them, Michael was sitting on the floor, quietly untwisting his kite, withdrawn into some private world she couldn't reach. He didn't have that noisy innocence Stephen had, of asking lots of questions, but seemed to have the silence of guilt.

"Come on, Michael," she said. "Reading practise. I'll be too tired to do it later," and reluctantly Michael collected his book and sat beside her on the settee. But it was as much a chore for her as it was for him, listening to him stumbling over the words of a book that bored her rigid. She kept correcting him, on every line, but he was bringing her to the brink of impatience. "For God's sake," she said suddenly. "What's wrong with you? Are you completely dim?" And at that point Andrew took over as Michael jumped off the settee, red-eared, and disappeared into the front room with his father. She heard slivers of more light-hearted tuition filtering through from time to time, and wondered where Andrew got the patience.

"I said, have you got anyone else to interview for your survey, Cheryl?" Marcia is brushing crumbs from her skirt and then she throws away her plastic sandwich packet, before tucking into her slimmers' yoghurt, black cherry flavour.

Cheryl looks up. "Yeah. Someone called Judd."

*

The files say Judd is a seasoned addict, late thirties, who blew his family inheritance on heroin many years back. Since then he's done everything: pharmacy break-ins, forged prescriptions, staged burglaries and insurance fiddles. He's an expert conner. Both Gina and Vernon have seen him out on the street with his checked cap, pulled well down over his eyes, and his walking stick, limping his phony limp. His GP believes in the semi-fictional injury, it is said, and merrily goes on prescribing Judd's favourite painkillers: DF118's.

Judd's place is on a down-at-heel high street, above a boarded-up shop. The smell of the place is what first hits Cheryl, as she follows Judd up the stairs. Sort of smoky and pissy, like old telephone boxes – the thick red sort that are almost obsolete. She shudders imperceptibly. As she follows him into the sitting-room, Judd says he's just this minute got back from the methadone clinic. "I've just met that new doctor. Dr Sharma. He's priceless, isn't he?" Cheryl realizes he's talking to a spaced-out girl on the sofa. "Yeah," says the girl with a slur in her voice. "A real soft touch. Phoned him up last week. The dog's spilt me meth over the carpet and lapped it up, I says, and he lapped it up and wrote me another script."

Judd roars with laughter. "Best thing since sliced bread."

Cheryl recognizes the girl now. She's that Nicky girl who was at 484 on the day of her interview, the one with the neolithic stones on her leather jacket. She's just noticed another bloke too, a black boy with dyed red hair, tough and bony, and their works are everywhere – bent blackened spoons and candles and foil – though she's learnt to show no reaction.

"I better sneak in some of your piss next time, Judd," says Nicky, grappling to keep her eyes ajar and her words from disintegrating into a sleepy heap, before gouching out. Her cup of coffee is about to soak her crotch, but Judd rescues it in time. "That's really taking the piss, that is," he says.

You see, it's dead easy to blag the doctors, he tells Cheryl, once he gets into the swing of the survey. The secret is to pretend you're not bothered whether they prescribe you anything or not. This is the advice I give to young impetuous addicts. Never look too desperate or you'll blow it. Never go into the surgery ranting or raving. You want the quack on your side, remember, so treat him with a bit of respect. Just say to him, all calm, like, how it's helped you before, the prescription.

He isn't exactly going straight, he says, but he's done so much time he wants to keep his nose clean. He regrets. He feels a sort of paternal responsibility toward these younger drug users and doesn't want them messing up their lives and bodies like he did. He doesn't want to be anyone's role model. You just get to a point in your life, he says. You get so fed up with it all and then you wake up one day and realize you just haven't got the taste for it like you used to.

She asks if they all use heroin. "Me and Nick do," says Judd. "Tone here does speed. So does Dodo – the other kid who lives here."

"Dodo does anything," says Tony.

"Yeah, but speed's his drug. Cuppa tea? Sorry, I've forgot your name."

"It's Cheryl. Yeah, that'd be great."

While Judd sorts out the tea, Tony, paranoid as a city, starts firing questions at her, demanding to know where the information is going. "I mean you come here wanting to know this and that but what have they ever done for me up there? Fuck all."

"This is why I'm here today," says Cheryl. "To find out what's lacking in our services."

"Services," sneers Tony. "You make it sound like a fuckin hotel."

"She's here to help, Tone," says Judd, returning with a drink for Cheryl.

Nicky, suddenly kindling to life from her post-heroin stupor, says, "Yeah and perhaps you wouldn't have sold my Sasha if you could have got a whatsit script."

"They'll never do that," says Tony. "It's just fuckin lip-service, ain it? And anyway I never sold no fuckin heap of china. It was that dodo upstairs done it."

"He never would. He was mad about Sasha same as me."

"Get real. He's a junkie same as the rest of us, ain he?"

They've got that oblivion of people used to rowing in public, Cheryl thinks, and then suddenly there's a great smash coming from above.

"Dodo on a bad trip again," says Judd, before limping off upstairs with his stick, and Cheryl takes it as her cue to leave.

8

It takes Dodo a while to find an Exchange & Mart and when he does the rumpled old woman there takes one look into his holey carrier bag, rattling with metal junk, and waves it away, like it was rotten cabbages. She's used to a better class of merchandise. You can see it in her face, and so he makes his way down town. The next Exchange & Mart looks grottier, more his sort of place, but the man in there just stands there without even looking in the bag. Sorry, no can do.

But he can't take his eyes off the man's hands. He'd kill for those juicy 3D veins. Strong feeder veins to carry traffic quick from A to B, no hold-ups.

"Didn't you hear me, sonny? I said do one."

"Just a fiver?"

"Look, I know your–"

"A coupla quid then."

"Two quid and that's your lot. I'm not likely to shift any of this, now on your bike, sonny."

 Perhaps he is a bit of a huckster, after all. His dad used to talk about the two of them going into business together, boating or angling or the like.

By the time he gets home, a bit more of the block up the road has been smashed to brick dust. Their house is still hanging in there, though the scaffolding's now all gone, making it feel bare and unprotected. The scaffolding could act as a shield too, sometimes.

He looks out from his room and sees how dense the rain is in the car headlights. He feels gloomy. There's an empty space and it's not just the scaffolding or the ironmonger empty space – it's Merlin. Merlin's had to go because he made his breathing worse and clogged his lungs but Merlin's gone somewhere good. To Annabel's. She's adopted him. She'll look after him. She's got puppies too. Do you want one, Dodo? They're going like hot cakes. He's thinking about it because dogs aren't as bad for his chest as cats.

He goes downstairs, puts the fire on, prepares his fix. He's just loosening his tourniquet, all done, when he hears the street door bang shut and Nicky's DM's thumping up the stairs. She comes in soaked, dries her hair, changes her clothes. Dangles her wet ones over a chair which steam in front of the fire.

"I'm getting one of Annabel's puppies, Nick."

"Yeah? It's not right without Merlin, is it?"

"I'm going round there."

"You could get a bird too while you're at it."

"What for?"

"Then I won't have to worry about you so much." She laughs, putting on her leather jacket with the neolithic stones painted on the back. "And I don't mean no feathered sort, neither."

"Oh, I can take care of myself, Nicky."

"Oi, sit down, will you? You're making me on edge jumping up and down all the time."

"Dogs just fit round your life. Maybe I'll get three. Maybe I should open an animal sanctuary."

"This place gets up my nose. The bugs are bugging me and I'm pissed off sharing my dinner with cockroaches."

"They're living creatures, Nicky, live and let live, eh? I mean they've gotta be more scared of you than you are of them."

"They carry disease, Stu said."

"You're supposed to be a veggie."

"Too right. You wouldn't catch me eating no cockroaches. Yuk."

"So? You gotta stand up for all creatures not just the fluffy ones, I'm telling you, they've got rights too, you've gotta work out just where you stand on cockroaches."

"On their fuckin' backs, that's where!"

*

he's all shook up
head's started jay-walking and dreaming of glastonbury
doesn't want to live inside his head so much
he's off out
never settles doesn't want to settle
life could be like stephen
alive!
don't come down
what have you lifted today
cheque books giros shops
whizzing past your window he sees you
cooking your hash
boiling your syringes
needle-freaks get to the point
now you're out of the frame

is he talking to anyone?

or himself?
who knows?
who cares?

*

Someone's rapping on the door. Rap rap rap. Hates rap. Wrap up.
He wants to sleep on but he can't because of the rapping and
everything's been trashed. Light bulbs and windows and shelves.
Merlin's paws will get shredded on the shattered glass but Merlin's
gone. Has there been a raid? The Old Bill? His old dealer?

"I can hear him. I think he's heard us at last." Nicky's voice.
"Unlock your door, Dodo. Quick. It's all right."

He feels a sharp pain in his right hand, all bandaged up. He feels
the eternal tremor in his body as he unlocks the door. "What the
fuck's going on?"

"It's the Pillocks . . . they heard all the noise before," says Nicky.
"They've got onto the landlord and he's on his way. He'll make us pay
for the damage. Come on, Dodo, we've got to get out."

"What noise?"

"It doesn't matter. You went off on one last night but it doesn't
matter."

"Off on one?"

"Yeah, you smashed the place up and locked yourself in your
room."

Off on one? So it was him – the glass and all. It might have been
the scaffolding-guns. Or the blade in his head. Or scary things in the
dark loft. He's wrecked the place and he doesn't remember. "Where
are we going?"

"Annabel said she could put us up for a few days."

*

At Annabel's, he gets to know some of the waif and stray dogs she's
taken in over the months. He coughs his pleurisy cough and feels the
sharp pain under his ribs and strokes Merlin again. All the puppies
have gone, but Annabel said he could have one of the other dogs.
He'll have that one there with the gentle nature, the black collie cross.
"I'm calling him Woodstock," he says, scoring some smack off her for
his cough and then he's off. Doesn't know where, but it's too crowded
at Annabel's and he doesn't want to cramp Nicky and Stu's style.

*

we're off to our new home, Woodstock
come on then
let's go
Midland Hotel, St Pancras

let's see if the door's still open like the geezer said

tis too
just climb over the plants on the stairs he said and carry on up
 like a church in here, Woodstock, a fucking cathedral, look at
those arched windows and pillars and things

look at this staircase
red walls all peeling
what's up, Woodstock?
look at all these rooms
come on in
listen to the echoes – my footsteps, the pigeons

hey, you can see the whole of fuckin London from this balcony,
Woodstock
you can really hear the pigeons
their wings cracking and whirring as they take off
we're gonna like it here, Woodstock
no one can get us here

lift's broken
staircase ain't safe neither
no one else is here, Woodstock
just you and me, eh?
folks have been here, mind, dumped their rubbish
cans
graffiti
matches
bones
people are fucked

I'm tired Woodstock

. . . .

must have crashed, did I?
didn't know I could still crash so quick
used to in school when I was tired from
 but I can't quite remember, Woodstock, weird how you shut
things away in the loft, eh?

nothing in the taps, Woodstock
bone dry, see?
don't worry I got us some bottled water
don't need to wash
who washes in this weather, eh?
hippies and hobos don't wash

just seen him, Woodstock
an old geezer sleeping in a pile of leaves through there
best leave him be

the biscuits are yours, Woodstock, and we'll share the water, yeah?

don't like the dark, Woodstock
gives me the spooks since Hell Hostel
wasn't no hostel, mind
told us it was a therapy centre, didn't they?
and I believed it, didn't I?
stupid cunt that I was

– it's time to put it behind you
– we're behind you all the way
– we'll keep you in the picture

they kept me in the fucking dark, Woodstock
made me look at videos
but it was lies
put me in their videos
there's some sick people around, Woodstock, I'm telling you
sick sick people

yeah, but we got each other now, ain't we?
no one can touch us here
we'll snuggle up under the blanket
hang on, Woodstock, hurts when I lie down
it's the pleurisy, see
but I got the gear
you tuck into the biscuits, Woodstock, and I'll chase the pain away
got a straw off that drink of orange
see?

not all soft, am I?

9

Nicky and Stu are his only visitors in hospital.

Sounds like pneumonia again, Nicky told him when he staggered back to Annabel's, a few weeks ago. In fact he's been treated for septicaemia and pneumonia – the one following from another. The nurses told him he's lucky to be alive.

But during his spell in hospital there's been a big change in Nicky and Stu. Nicky's been in for detox and Stu's clean too. They've chucked out all their old druggie stuff: needles, battered old spoons, citric acid, the lot. Even stuff you wouldn't think of, like records that remind them, or the cushion Nicky used to press tight against her, rocking, groaning, soaking. Waiting for a miracle. It's all been bagged up and binned, she said, and now Stu's aunt's gone and bought Stu a flat, hasn't she? Well, she's no kids of her own so she likes to treat him. Sunk all her money into it. A proper flat in Islington with mod cons, and Nicky and Stu said that when Dodo comes home from hospital, he's coming to live with them, no buts.

Being in hospital has stabilized him, too. It's forced him to keep off the drugs, except prescribed ones, so perhaps it'll be a new start for them all, he thinks as he sets foot in Stu's new pad a few days later. The flat is on the first floor of a small block called Buckingham Court, overlooking a courtyard with stone tubs and a few scrawny saplings, still tied to their stakes. Inside, there are flouncy net curtains, pine wardrobes, nowhere to put your muddy boots. Everything is fitted, nothing scuffed. He prefers things that rattle a bit. Things you can endlessly dismantle and rebuild.

There's only one bedroom, so he sleeps in the lounge with the wide window where he can meditate on changes of light and weather. Cuts of rain on the window-pane. Shifting colours of streetlamps.

Stu's aunt (his great aunt really) is a rich widow in her seventies who means well and has a good grasp of drugs for someone her age, but believes anything Stu tells her. Lucky for her, then, that Stu and Nicky really mean to make a fresh go of it. Stu gets a job delivering pizzas and the three of them only smoke dope in the evenings now, nothing else. They lie low, watching videos and playing cards. Even a bit of reading. Well, he does anyway – The Hobbit and Mervyn Peake and King Arthur – things he's always wanted to read.

Then one night, Nicky suggests they go clubbing. They go once, twice, and then it starts creeping up until it's every Friday and Saturday night. They come home to the icy feel of 4 am and their forgotten underwear, frozen stiff as a board on the communal balcony.

By February, Annabel has hunted them down. She drives over like a bloke in her old banger. She comes first with videos. Rumour has it they aren't using any more, she says, and their squeaky-clean existence seems to back this up. Well, we're still snorting a bit of this and that, Stu lies. Better Annabel think they're still dabbling a bit, otherwise she might swoop right in. But she's patient and it works. She finds the chink in Nicky's armour, because Nicky's the one to go for. Nicky's the one to cave in first; who won't say no to the odd freebie.

And then Stu starts getting a taste for it too, just like Annabel planned. Stu was never much into the gear before, not like Nicky. It's only chasing, he says, but before long he and Nicky are sharing works and Stu has to pack in his job delivering pizzas. His old aunt becomes ill and so her visits tail off. On the rare occasions she does call, she gives Stu fair warning as she doesn't want a wasted visit and thereby giving him time to lock away his new scales and other drug dealing paraphernalia.

And the scales are tipping. One minute there's nothing but balance, the next minute Stu's aunt's had a stroke and is confined to a hospital bed which is all too convenient. Carte blanche to do as they please. They're junkies for fuck's sake. They'll sell your granny. They've moved in, and Dodo finds he can't dream out at the streetlights any more. The scales are tipping lower still and nor can he get in the bathroom when he wants. It's always locked for years at a time because of some hard line mainliner digging around for the best of a bad bunch. It always stinks of diarrhoea in there or piss. Everyone pissing in the sink or the bath, pools of it on the floor.

He's been banging away on the bathroom door and now something's happening at long last. The woman who falls out is still locked in somewhere. It's not that they don't see eye to eye, it's that they don't see each other at all but he's been waiting to go in, he's been banging and banging and now it's his turn to hog it, do what he has to do.

The loo's blocked as always. He flushes it, a pointless thing because the bloody swabs and pieces of loo roll – smeared brown and disintegrating like a failed poached egg – swirl high under the rim, it's all about to overflow and this is him too. Full of muck which keeps coming up and whirling around and won't flush away and in it goes, in the shit goes to the body and out the shit comes from the mind, and he sees the lipstick words on the mirror. RIP Connor, it says. RIP my little baby, so it was *that* woman who was in here before. Nettie, Nettie whatsherface, everyone knows about her, about Connor. Nettie was high, so the story goes, high as a kite when she stirred the soup that day, the soup cooking on the stove which she turned off just before she fell, fell to the floor, she's always falling, stupid cow, lay where she fell, out cold while her little Connor walks right out of the house to get some help for his mummy who's fallen down, walks down the path onto the busy road in front of a car, splat, bye-bye Connor, and Nettie's high all the time now, higher than kites, can't live with the guilt, but she isn't high really, she's one of those kites that won't stay up, that go plummeting into trees or down at your feet in a tangled mess, cluck cluck what a head-fuck and there was a man lying in a heap and they keep playing that Cream record, the neighbours want us out, this used to be such-a-nice-neighbourhood, dirty plates all over the floor, and the scales have tipped as low as they can, filthy scum, and syringes in the tubs which they sling out of the window and the same record playing over and over all day and all night, in a white room, and there's a big-dick gun sticking out the mirror, come to get You, and the writing's on the wall and the mirror, and they're still playing our song in a white room with black curtains and there was that old man lying in a heap of leaves and no one's clapped eyes on the electric-light-girl lately so her bulb must have blown out in the end she was switched on too soon turn that fuckin record off it's a real head-fuck and none of it's psychedelic except the flowery curtains i pulled down but not black curtains perhaps i'm the electric-light-girl get me out of this headspace got to clutch my head and there's a zillion eyes looking out at you the gun shot them there and the buzz in your head you're going down the dark chute onto the blade which is blunt and just a bit more for mr ray and then you can get up and play and turn that fuckin there was an old man with maggots lying in a heap of leaves in my home in st pancras dead as a dodo soaked in rain or old piss he made woodstock cry and shiver but you can cut yourself alive but the blade doesnt cut cutthroat take a cut shes cut up cut herself up cut him off cut you out cut it with glucose with rat poison i don't half fancy some chips with piles of salt and the buzz is coming zzzz zzzz zzzz in waves in my ears let me in youve been in there hours in a white room where the shadows run from themselves

they're still falling in through the front door one two eight at a
time those two brothers carry a gun they say but this is the contraflow
going down and out across the courtyard

bang bang i'm almost shot away
almost had my chips

REDUCE   SPEED   NOW

10

On the street you're your own boss. You don't have to answer to nothing or no one. He thinks this as he pushes Woodstock around in the old sixties pram he nicked from outside some junk shop. Woodstock and his worldly possessions: a couple of maggoty blankets, some holey socks, a stack of old newspapers and a few polluted vegetables scavenged from outside greengrocers or rich dustbins. You have to overcome pride and taboo, raiding dustbins, and now it's a piece of cake. Now he's crossed that border into that other world. That colder, shadier side of life and it's okay.

They stare at the pram. Some of them laugh. He barely speaks to a soul. He doesn't want people near him, but has the pigeons eating out of his hand, three at a time. Or flapping about his shoulders in their hundreds. Trafalgar Squareish. He comes here most days. Sits. Thinks. Walks to his bench. Comes over all sleepy. This is his sleeping time. Sleep by day, walk by night. Conserve your energy. Protect yourself from danger. Protect yourself from cold. The weather's getting warmer, but it never quite warms him. The wind still comes in. He's always cold. Always damp. From the inside out. But the sun on his blanket defrosts him.

Just give us a bench in the sun, eh Woodstock? And we're happy as Larry.

On his bench he'll listen to the buskers playing their tin whistles. He wishes he could play like that.

Then he'll lie down, Woodstock up against him, keeping him company, keeping him warm. He'll close his eyes awhile, the background coming and going like radio waves. Then he'll lose it to sleep. Scrappy sleep. Then he'll wake up, bleary, and the whole scene will have shifted, moved on.

On wet days, he finds places to shelter. Drop-in centres. Soup kitchens. Places where you can get a cheap hot meal with the pennies in your pocket. Places filled with folk like him. Surviving from night to night, café to café, shelter to shelter. Folk you can share a cup of coffee with, a fag, a couple of hours of your time. Because that's something everyone's got stacks of. There's that old Irish lady who's going a bit dotty. Tells you her life story as she picks the fish out of her teeth and wipes them on the trousers she's been wearing all winter long. Then there's that Lottie woman with her fake fur and Mary Poppins brolley, her supermarket trolley full of cheap bright charity-shop clothes. You can be who you like here. You can throw away your old self and get a new one. There's folk out here got nothing but they'll give you their last penny. They'll tell you the best way to build your cardboard house, the best place. They'll tip you off about the best loos or shelters to spend the night in and there's another sort of folk who won't tell you. They've only got a little and they want to keep it for themselves. They don't want to share. They hoard. It's the law of the jungle out here. He's like this. You get on with your life and leave me to get on with mine. He's good at slipping between people. Strength is distance, the little dream-girl said. Then there's the folk hanging out in gangs. Just another society with codes, but they've got something he needs so he hovers. Like a low-flying wasp, until he finds what he's looking for. Drugs. Speed enough to raise his spirits, to keep him awake at the right times. Speed costs money, but he can't cope with signing on, with keeping appointments at set times. There's a quicker and easier way. Crouching down in a disused doorway with your 'hungry and homeless' card and black cap upturned, Woodstock in the pram. Woodstock brings in the pounds. Folk don't like the thought of hungry dogs, even if they don't care much for hungry people.

He never looks up. He says his quiet thank-yous to the ankles of the good-hearted, but today there's this man squatting down to his level, right in his face. He's wearing a bright-coloured open shirt. Hint of an accent. Australian? South African? Never was much good on accents.

"Hi, I'm Neil. Nice hound you've got yourself there. What's his name?"

"Woodstock."

"Woodstock, eh? You're a bit young to remember it, aren't you?"

He doesn't trust this too-familiar stuff, all this petting Woodstock shit. He wants Neil to fuck out of his face.

"I've seen you before, haven't I? Can't forget that pram. You live in cardboard city, right?"

"Don't live in no city."

"So, what's worse than waking up in your own piss?" Neil waits for an answer, but getting none, answers it himself. "Waking up in someone else's. I'd get pissed off if people kept pissing over my home."

"Can't do nothing about it. You just gotta get on and make another."

"Hey, you're quite enterprising you people, aren't you? I mean, people say you lot don't want a roof over your head but that's bollocks, isn't it? I mean, if I offered you one you'd take it, right?"

"Depends."

"On what?"

"The catch."

"If there was no catch."

"There's gotta be."

"What would you say if I offered you a place to live as long as you wanted?"

"There's gotta be a catch."

"My friend's looking for someone who'll work for him."

"What sorta work? I ain't never worked."

"There's nothing to it and you get somewhere to live."

"Oh yeah?"

"Yeah, you get to live in the flat above me," says Neil, shiftily opening his tobacco pouch, just enough to flaunt the concealed little packages inside. "So? Still say no?"

He's drooling. Neil's got him this time. He can't turn this one down. They want him to run for them most like – Neil and this other geezer – in return for a roof over his head and food in his stomach and enough drugs to see him through.

*

And now he's forever wired, shaking like a jelly, spin-dryer thoughts waiting to be unplugged. Can't-walk-straight legs, giving-way legs. Someone's gonna gun him down, all those people he owes, going back years, all out there somewhere, and someone was shot away at Buckingham Court but not Nicky or Stu or it was the buzz in his head, the blade in his thoughts always cutting.

Feels drop-dead tired

Never awake in the unsafety of his room

Toxic jaundiced room

Hey aqualung

Today is Saturday. Mr G day.

You never know with Mr G. He might be sitting on a chair. He can pop out any time anywhere. From curtains and wardrobes and mirrors but Mr G hasn't waited today. Must be off on some other business today, but Mr G's left a little package on the bed…

This is all he needs. He wishes it was all in vein but he can't find his works. There was a 2 ml barrel in the bathroom, there fuckin was. Some cunt's nicked it. Got to have it now. Drugs without works is like fags without matches. Worse. With fags you can always ask for a light. Fuck sake.

Finds a barrel in the cabinet, a bit bent but it'll do. He sits on the loo, tries to slow his breathing. In, one two three, out, one two three. He's trying to get a vein, trying so hard it hurts. You can always find a vein, Dodo. That's what Nicky's always said. Can you find us one? Girls are different like that, different types of veins, sort of fainter, but his are all packing up, he's going to have to try down below, and he can hear the key in the bedroom door. He'll never get it in now, he's frozen up, because Mr G can walk straight from the bedroom into here. There's no bathroom lock any more, you can see the marks where it used to be.

Mr G is short and stocky with cropped hair and a scar on his left cheek and a high-pitched snigger but he isn't dressed in his suit today, he's in T-shirt and shorts. So is Neil who's standing behind him and Mr G's brought the nasty camera again which probes you with its third eye, head-on, over its three legs.

He drops his syringe and Mr G stands on it.

He's on the floor, going wild. "Gimme it."

"Gimme it?" taunts Mr G. "That's no way to ask, is it? I'm afraid you haven't earned it yet. This horrid thing under my foot – I've got an idea."

"Let him have it," says Neil. "Don't be cruel. He's in a state."

"And look at the state of my flat which he's turned into a cowshed. In fact, doesn't he remind you of a filthy cow, that lets itself be pushed around from here to there? No horns, you see. You never allowed yourself to sink this low, Neil, I'll say that for you. You were reformable. But as he's always too out of it I've had to send the newest recruit out instead to do my drop-offs."

"Come on, Mr G, let's go."

"You want to go, then go, but me and the druggie still have outstanding business to settle – he has to pay for the roof over his head. They all have a street value, just like the filth they pump themselves with. Nothing comes for free."

*

just do as I say and you won't get hurt, we're just taking advantage of the son and you're looking a bit below pa today, and the hot lamps shine in his face and blind him like the dark, his button and his flies they're undone, just do it, don't fuck about, you were about to do it anyway, that's what those big barrels are for, injecting in your groin, well, aren't they, let's see you do it, let's capture it on camera, that's the way, that's great, look at the camera lovely now let's have one of you looking down, great, and he doesn't want to remember but he is remembering mr ray is lonely mrs ray isn't good to him will you help mr ray like you did last time then we can go fishing and you still owe me for one weeks rent so see you at the same time tomorrow then we'll be more or less up to date and he's exceeded his speed limit

*

can't do it no more, the blade's getting blunt,
neil has to do it, neil or mister g, got to give him his jabs round the clock
just to keep him from   drooping,
from crashing

like a dead duck

picking up pieces of his broken
living from fix to fix, just the feel of needle
the sear of pain
and the blade's getting
blunt

neil will fix it, neil or mister g, his hypodermic hit men,
feels like a pincushion or voodoo doll, going round and round
spin-dryer head
stuck in a revolving door being whizzed nowhere

theres space   between   the   w o r d s

feeling like a dead duck
picking up pieces of his broken

it comes and goes
in radio waves

don't go to the loft

REHAB

1

The Research Assistant, Sarah Samuels, appointed to 484 back in September, wasted no time in making her presence felt early on in her new post, much to Cheryl's annoyance. Twenty years younger than Cheryl, Sarah Samuels has done an MSc in Research Methodology or some such thing and has her name on several articles, which have appeared in prestigious journals. This means she's accomplished at drafting research proposals and can design a convincing questionnaire at the drop of a hat. What's more, she's completely computer literate. Her eventual aim is to be a Clinical Psychologist she tells her colleagues who are all suitably impressed. Neither does Vernon lose an opportunity to remind everyone just how lucky they are to have someone of Sarah's calibre working at 484 and he, for one, will be encouraging her all he can to develop her own research projects.

Very quickly, Cheryl no longer feels herself to be the in-house expert – she is, after all, just a Team Assistant, and people who want more thorough explanations of this or that go to Sarah. Not only that, but Sarah beavers away in the office till well past Mrs Jenkins' cleaning of the firedoors most nights and, it is said, even takes research papers home to read.

Cheryl's only hope is that where Sarah is super-efficient with statistics and theories, she will come a cropper when it comes to the clients: she won't be streetwise enough or she'll have a bad attitude or she'll be regarded with suspicion because she looks too academic or out of touch. But not a bit of it. Sarah's empathic in all the right places. She's confident, witty, kind, firm – utterly chameleon, utterly sickening. She's got the personal touch, you can see it in evidence all round the office where she's stamped her personality with carefully tended plants and funny cartoon strips and her own mug.

When Sarah does make the occasional error she does it with impunity – it never seems to dent her overall integrity. Oh rats, she will say, opening up her diary at the rubberband marker, I've double-booked for Thursday at three. Sarah can afford to throw caution to the wind. She can make a virtue of her unreliability, and Cheryl feels it like a slap in the face because now all the interesting stuff, like attending conferences and forums and meeting other experts in the field – even interviewing the clients – is given to Sarah, while Cheryl is forced to return to hours and hours of number-crunching and pie charts and typing letters.

"I'm taking two weeks holiday," she announces one day in November, at rather short notice, but two weeks holiday will give her a chance to sit back and take stock.

*

Cheryl watches through the window as Elaine, now twenty-three and black-haired, shuffles past the stone penguins and through the damp leaves strewn up the long drive to Tea Rose Cottage. Elaine is holding Juliet's hand, and at five years old, Juliet could almost be Elaine's daughter.

Elaine has now got herself a new flat and job in Bournemouth. She's the only one who acts as a link between the two families: old and new.

Cheryl joins Elaine outside, barely aware of Juliet, now running about and squealing in the leaves.

"The new girl at work I was telling you about. She can only be about your age."

Elaine coughs and blows her nose. "So what are you gonna do about it?"

"I don't know yet."

But deep inside she knows a change is due. Sarah is forcing her arm, is creating change, just as the pregnancy did back then, those six years ago. "Pregnant?" said Luigi. "A little bambino? You'll have to come and join me in Bournemouth now."

She did, it was a new start, away from the disaster that was her marriage and family back in London, and Juliet came along the following spring, like a damp new bud, and Cheryl remembered again that new-baby feeling, like the one she'd had with Elaine. A heady-pink feeling that makes your whole world rock.

And then there's the other sort of change, the one that creeps along as they grow. "Why don't you go back to being a full time mother?" says Elaine, coughing and sneezing out the germs she's brought with her.

"Don't be daft. Juliet's fine with her Luigi and her stepmother…and could you not keep coughing near me…I don't want to get that germ. This is meant to be my holiday."

"Oh that's charming, that is." Elaine lights a cigarette, just to be arsy, Cheryl presumes. "It's great to see you too." Then she clatters off upstairs in the dormer bedroom, fogging the place with her smoke. Cheryl hates Elaine when she's like this. She's like a squally adolescent, and Cheryl wonders what happens to that innocent spark of children. When does it leave them? Eleven? Nine? How does it leave them? Through their pubescent pores? And where does it go? Wherever it goes, it goes for good.

Cheryl cups Juliet's face within her hands, and thinks, I've been such a lousy mother to this little one. But the novelty wore off again, didn't it? Juliet grew too fast, she sucked and chewed and pulled, she popped up all over the house like a jack-in-the-box, and the words came in thick and fast like teeth, soon to bite, and then where was all the romance she'd hoped for with Luigi? At the same time, she peered into each passing pram with a rapacious envy, especially if they contained the new sticky-pup sort with a pearly ear, tucked well down below a row of plastic ducks or pretty pom-poms ...

2

"Well," says Callum, whose room Michael shares. "You've survived the first day which is the worst day. It's uphill all the way from now on, kid."

Michael isn't convinced, though all the folk here at Chrysalis seem friendly enough. Except he didn't like the way that Jeff bloke stood over him while he unpacked. Well, they've got to check for drugs, haven't they? It's a rehab, isn't it? A big old house in the country, with goats and herb gardens and art studios and things. When he first arrived he was taken into Anthea's office. She's the woman in charge here: a large, maternal woman with soft curly hair. But there are loads of rules: all incoming post to be opened by staff, no cash handling, no going out unaccompanied, no visits or phone calls during the first week. Worse than prison. He doesn't remember being told any of this before he came. Not that he's expecting any visitors. The only people who might have visited are Nicky and Stu and he's lost touch with them.

And he can't get used to being called Michael – it makes him feel like a kid again. Dodo's fun, you can't take it too seriously, but Michael…

At least Woodstock's with him and he's seen another dog and a couple of cats roaming about. He asked Anthea whose they were and she told him the cats used to be Shona's, but they've become the community's pets now, everyone looks after them. He vows they'll not do that with Woodstock. They've been through a lot together, him and Woodstock, and he's the only one who knows his ways.

When he first sat in Anthea's office, he didn't want to leave. He felt sort of protected, but she stood up, swinging that stack of keys, and took him straight to the lion's den. He wouldn't have minded if she'd have stayed at his side, but she was suddenly whisked away, wanted on the phone or something, just when he was right there in the doorway, so he was left to fend for himself.

A group of strangers when you're not out of your box – is there anything scarier? He felt like he'd just stepped off a merry-go-round as he walked in the coffee lounge. But there was this bloke, a bit older than him, with a pink nose and a strawberry-blond ponytail, playing patience by the window. That was Callum, and Callum took him under his wing right away. Said they'd be sharing rooms.

"Nothing beats it, eh Michael?" says Callum now, in his broad Scottish. "A bed with clean sheets."

*

They're treating him gently, because he's still in his first week. He's been ill most of it – that and dead sleepy. Drugs must be good for him if he's so ill without them.

When he can, he staggers to the window and gazes out through the bare January trees at the men's re-entry house – Oak Tree Lodge – where men come and go as they please. It looks a long way off. He'll never make it there, that's for sure. He's only made it this far because he's too ill to do a runner. But as soon as he's better he's off. At least being ill has got him out of all those intense groups and finishing off that video thing which made him freak a bit. Maybe they'll forget about it, with any luck.

And there's so many new people to take in. Anthea, and Jeff with the beard, and Faith with the dreadlocks, longer than his, proper thin dreads because she's black. His key worker, she said, whatever that is. They're the staff. Then there are the other residents – Lesley, Shona with the big bust and tattoos, Vanessa with the shades, big Barry with the red face, Ronnie who looks pretty lean and mean.

When he's well enough, he shuffles about the house in long jumpers, his joints all aching, and people bring him sweet coffee and wish him well, but he feels that low he would happily top himself if he could be arsed. He would do it quietly. In some derelict barn somewhere. Only he doesn't have the energy. And, anyway, they don't let you out of their sight for five minutes here. They call it support. He calls it hounding, though he can't tell them that. They read to him from books. They read him like a book. You look a bit down, Michael. Want to talk? Don't worry, everyone who's used speed for that long goes through what you're going through now. It just takes time for the mind and body to adjust, that's all. Your system's probably been crying out to be flushed out – like a defrosted fridge – so it can work more efficiently. Talk to us. Any of us. That's what we're here for.

They bug him with questionnaires. To keep his mind busy, though they give other reasons. They say questionnaires are a good way of focussing on areas to be addressed in counselling. They leave him to fill them out on his own. *Please indicate whether you have recently felt any of the following – anger, depression, tension, anxiety, sleeplessness – by ticking the appropriate box: frequently, sometimes, occasionally, never.*

All of them, all of the time.

*

Lesley Sweet knocks on the office door where Faith and Anthea are discussing the progress of one of the other residents. "I thought I'd let you know," says Lesley, her eyes wide and worried-looking. "Michael's just walked out of the art session. I think it was because he thought Dennis didn't much go for the fantasy piece he was painting."

"Thank you, Lesley." Anthea waits for Lesley to leave before turning to Faith. "Dennis may be a retired art teacher, but he's pretty hopeless when it comes to encouraging our new residents, don't you think? What we really need is an Art Therapist."

"It wouldn't be so bad if Michael had had some proper counselling," says Faith. "Or the chance to air his doubts and fears, but everything's had to be put back because he's been ill." She gets to her feet. "Excuse me, won't you, but I think I better look for him. People have walked right out of here over less."

But Michael isn't in his room. He isn't with the goats and chickens as she'd hoped. She follows the short cut through the wooded area to the main road, this being the most likely route to take, and there he is, bag packed, Woodstock at his feet, trying to hitch a ride. But others before him have been glad she's caught them in time.

"Is this what you really want, Michael? If it is, I'll turn back now and leave you alone. But I thought you might want to talk things through first, just to make sure."

"I can't do it."

She smiles. "Everyone's felt like you're feeling, believe me." Then she says, "Why don't you come back and give it one more crack, eh? Then if it doesn't work out, at least you'll know you've given it your best shot." He looks relieved. As if, although he didn't want to stay, neither did he really want to leave.

She takes him somewhere quiet to talk back at the house. This won't be a proper counselling session today, she tells him, placing two coffees down on the table. His is the one with four sugars. She knows this is probably why so many of them have dental problems, but she never bats an eyelid at the number of spoonfuls – she knows all about the sweet tooth of the addict and their need for comfort through sugar. She's been there.

She notices the quiver in his fingers and face muscles with each drag of his cigarette. Today will be more of an ice-breaking session, a getting to know each other session, except she knows he'll probably learn more about her than she will about him. Because it takes time to build up sufficient trust in your key worker, that's only natural, so she'll stick with safe things for today. She'll tell him how the counselling works, she'll talk about goal-setting and ground rules, she'll hammer home the issues around confidentiality. And she'll let him know that she's unshockable – that she's heard everything there is to hear. She'll stick with the present, for now, though she knows he, like all of them, carries a past – one that drags him down from behind.

But after a few sessions, Michael's still not opening up. He's still saying Fine or No Problem to her every question – no matter how she phrases it – that relates to his background: his parents, his schooldays, his adolescence. She's seen this before and it rings alarm bells. She needs to find a way in, just one route, to get at the buried injury. After four or five sessions she decides to take a risk, otherwise he'll play his evasive games indefinitely.

"Look, Michael...I know it's difficult. I know it's probably the most difficult thing you'll ever have to do, but everyone who's ever made it here has first to deal with their past before they can move forward. That can take a long time and a lot of hard work, but those who've done it say it's empowering. It's enabled them to take charge of their lives again. It's up to you."

"Yeah, but I ain't got nothing to say."

"Would you find it easier to write it down perhaps?"

"I ain't got nothing to write. I can make something up if that's what you want."

"No, it's not what I want," she says. "I'm just trying to help you to communicate, and memories are a good start. You must have some memories about growing up, even if they're only neutral ones."

"Nothing worth mentioning."

"Okay," she says. "I'm not going to push you if you're not ready, but I will say this. I've seen people time and time again, sitting exactly where you're sitting now, and still holding back in their second or third or fifth week, but there hasn't been a single one of them who hasn't had something to offload. We had one guy, he's left now, let's call him Charlie. Anyway, this Charlie said when he was first here that it was like being constipated, and show me an addict who doesn't know what that feels like!" (He is, at least, smiling now). "Anyway, he said, this Charlie, that it's like having this nasty dark mess inside you and it's been there so long you have to heave and strain to get any of it out, and sometimes you even need medical intervention – that's where you come in, Faith, he said – but what a relief once it's out! In the words of Charlie – even just a little bit at a time can bring enormous relief! You have a think about it anyway,

Michael."

Michael lies awake through Callum's sleep murmurings. He's not even tired. It's not as if he doesn't like Faith, she's nice and funny and everything, and he would like to make it easy for her. That's why he's lying here doing his best to dredge up something positive from his schooldays, like she's told him to do. This is his task before his next session. He really is trying, but nothing's springing to mind. School was even worse than home, with those frightening dinner ladies and their ladles – full of disgusting custard – waiting to smother his Bakewell tart, or those monitors snapping at him to eat up quick because he was toying with the food on his plate. It was a delaying tactic he used during First Sitting to cut short that endless shapeless time in the playground afterwards. He still smells it, that middle-of-the-day smell of stewed beef and fear and wanting to Go Home For Dinners. He wonders whether it was that much better for Stephen at his swanky school, but Stephen could fit in anywhere. Stephen was clever and sociable.

He wonders what Stephen's doing now. University probably. Stephen will make it to university, their mother used to say. He can picture her two faces: one for each of them. The face of pride for Stephen and the face of disappointment for him. Sometimes you're an embarrassment to me, Michael, she would say, and it would leave a fine cut, like sharp paper, drawing blood without warning.

He falls into a dream and his mother's there already. She takes on huge dimensions, she's taken it over, hijacked even his dreams.

*

– Did you like painting at school, Michael?
– I used to.
– Until?
– I dunno.
– Did someone put you off?
– Maybe.
– Who?
– Teachers, I s'pose.
– Why was that?
– Dunno. Always criticizing, weren't they?
– Would you say that you're easily put off things?
– Dunno. S'pose so.
– Why do you think that is?
– I lose interest, don't I?
– You lose interest when there's no encouragement, is that it?

– Something like that.

– Did you feel any of your efforts were praised at school?

– Don't remember. Wasn't there that much.

– What about at home? Were you praised for your efforts there?

– Sometimes.

– Who praised you at home?

– My dad.

– Your dad. And what would he praise you for?

– This and that. Can't think of anything off the top of my head.

– And your mum? Would she praise you?

– No.

– She didn't praise you when you did something well?

– No.

– Why do you think that was?

– Dunno. I didn't do nothing that well, I s'pose.

– Everybody does something well at some time or other. Perhaps it wasn't her way to praise people.

– She praised my brother.

– And how did that make you feel?

– That he was better than me, I s'pose.

– What was the effect on you, do you think, when you didn't receive any praise from your mother for things you felt you did well?

– How d'you mean?

– Well, did it make you try all the more, for instance, or just give up?

– Give up, I s'pose.

– Do you still feel like that today? That there's no point in really trying at something because you'll not get any encouragement anyway?

– I haven't really thought about it.

– Well, to put it another way, do you think your feelings today may be linked to your early experiences?

– I dunno.

– Well at Chrysalis we don't believe in comparing people unfavourably with others. Everyone's got strengths and skills, and our job is to guide and encourage you. Help you find the things that you like doing, because these are the things that we tend to do well, yes?

– Yeah. Can we finish now? My head's banging.

3

Faith twiddles with her dreadlocks at the team meeting. Jeff is saying how he's had a long talk with Vanessa about her shades. "It's a power thing, of course. Vanessa can see others, but they can't see her. She feels vulnerable and exposed without them, but she's agreed to take them off at certain times. Can I suggest we all give her lots of positive encouragement by telling her how nice it is to see her eyes and that sort of thing? Without overdoing it, of course."

Jeff turns to Faith. "Pity you're not her key worker, Faith. Don't you still need someone as a case study? For your counselling course? She'd make a good subject."

"Actually, I would like Michael for my case study," she says. "Though I feel it might be counter-productive to tape-record our sessions at this stage. We'll see."

Anthea, always a bit over-protective towards the residents, is looking concerned. "Michael? Do you think that's a good idea?"

"Well, I haven't raised the possibility with him yet, because it's important that I approach it in the right way – I don't want him to be suspicious of it getting into the wrong hands or anything."

A faint furrow appears between Anthea's brows. "This is what concerns me. You'll remember what he was like about the introductory video."

Faith nods. "It is fragile with him at the moment…sometimes I feel as if we're really starting to get somewhere and then suddenly we're back to square one."

"Oh that's not unusual. Tell me, is he participating more in the activities?"

Faith shakes her head. "Not fully, no. And he's not doing his turn on teas and coffees."

"Quiet lad, isn't he?" says Jeff.

"On the outside maybe," says Faith. "But there's a lot of noise on the inside, if you get my drift."

"What, sort of passive-aggressive?" says Jeff, though Faith doesn't respond, because she doesn't like that expression.

Instead, she says, "It's a real shame because he's such a nice kid underneath."

Jeff fiddles with his beard thoughtfully. "Do you think he's been abused, Faith?"

"I'm certain of it. All the classic signs are there," she says. "But I don't want to push him too hard. Timing is everything."

She thinks how retrospective it can all become, because children who are suffering today, right now, don't have the means of expression. They have to wait for the scrutiny and revision and distortion of hindsight, and she is hopeful things will change in this age of information and awareness; with these TV programmes that always seem to have close-up shots of empty swings, or rocking horses, and a music box tinkling out a nursery rhyme ...

4

Michael sees himself as a daddy-long-legs which keeps bashing against the same old light – a light that keeps burning him, a light that'll kill him soon if he doesn't learn from experience. But this time he has learnt, hasn't he? This time it's different because – after his brief binge at Annabel's (where he was hoping to catch up with Nicky and Stu but discovered they've moved to Hastings) – he very quickly lost the taste for drugs. He's now kipping on Judd's floor, but he's seen the light. The Chrysalis light. He's been thinking about Chrysalis, about the people there and the books and the goats and the gentle meditation.

And Callum.

He and Callum were sitting on Callum's bed playing first noughts and crosses, and then Hangman with sixties and seventies bands or artists. Callum put his arm round him, but it didn't feel odd. "I give up with this one, Michael," he said. "Blank E Blank E Blank I Blank." Then he ran his hand down Michael's back to the waistband of his jeans and round the front. "If you want me to stop, Michael, just say." Callum then undid Michael's flies and slipped his hand in, and Michael felt the thrill as they touched; as they tossed each other off fast and furious. But the next day he felt confused and ran, even though they didn't do anything that bad. But it was the secrecy. The hush-hush. The breaking of rules. That made it wrong, but he misses Callum's broad Scottish, his little wisdoms on life, his smell, his closeness. He's thought about Faith too. She's pretty sound. She persuaded him to pick up the tin whistle. She could have helped him, though he'd started to dread the way she filled his silences with those intimate questions, the way she was getting nearer and nearer to the dark loft …but if he ever finds the strength to tell her it would all evaporate out there instead of solidifying inside like ancient poison. He's through with guilt-edged thoughts. In fact, his thoughts feel a lot different lately. Sort of more together. He's even thought of something positive from his schooldays, it came to him just the other day, out of the blue. He was fifteen, and had a girlfriend of sorts – Louise – who he walked home from school or took to the pictures on Saturdays. She didn't fit in either. They saw each other for a few months, he even sat a couple of his O Levels, school being a positive time then. But then his father put her off on the phone, made out Michael was unavailable, hinting that he had another girlfriend, so she dumped him. He only found this out later, after he'd left home and bumped into her – the day the O Level results were due out. They walked to the school together, but she already had another boyfriend by this time...

But he realizes he wants to tell Faith about the good things.

And Faith can be funny, she can put a smile on your face, for sure, like that time she said about constipation.

Perhaps now's the time. Perhaps now he's ready to see it through if they'll have him back.

After work, Cheryl crunches along the gravel drive to Tea Rose Cottage, past the hedges and the penguin bird bath, and puts her key in the door. She opens the fridge and warms up the third quarter of a Safeway's quiche and pours herself a glass of Chardonnay. She likes her independence, and the convenience meals, reminding her how busy her life is, no time for domestics. Up there, in the cupboard, there's months' worth of dark sticky rings left by bottles of soy sauce and camp coffee and tins of syrups. She won't let some wet-eared graduate spoil all that, oh no.

Ever since her fortnight off in November, and a further week at Christmas, Cheryl realizes just how restless she's become at 484. It's the boring secretarial tasks, it's the tedious statistics, it's Sarah Samuels creaming off the best projects.

After her food, she puts some final stitches to her present tapestry, a rather twee arrangement of flowers, and thinks about Stephen who will graduate in the summer. Time is creeping steadily. She has money in the bank, money she's saved from work and her share of the sale of the house she shared with Andrew. He kept the house on after they split up, so their children would have a base, but since they have all gone there was no need to keep it on any longer, although that's not the sole reason he decided to sell. He's met someone else and his new partner wanted them to start afresh. She didn't want reminders of his life before. Cheryl can't say she blames her but it makes her wonder whether she should have insisted on the house sale earlier and bought a place herself: a two-bedroomed flat, say, where Stephen could come and stay. Not that he couldn't stay here – after all, it's never stopped Elaine – but Stephen rarely calls her nowadays. She understands. All his minutes and hours are accounted for, as are hers.

And there's this other thought, shifting about like a cat that won't settle on your lap. Earlier at work today, instead of ignoring the usual openings and new job opportunities that get circulated from time to time, she took down details of one in particular.

It's at a drug rehabilitation centre in Hampshire called The Chrysalis Trust, currently advertizing for a Day Worker. OK, it's with the same client group and not exactly the ideal career move but it could add to her CV and she is suitably qualified now. She lays down the tapestry and walks over to Janet's writing bureau where she finds some top-quality writing paper, perfect for a letter of application.

6

Michael now shares his room with Barry. It's for the best, they said. He and Callum have had to back off emotionally, pretend it didn't happen, be distant with each other. Because there are rules at Chrysalis about Exclusive Relationships. There are rules about sex in the house, like there are rules about drugs in the house, though sex is treated more leniently than drugs. Drugs in the house means instant dismissal.

There are other things starting to happen, anyway, which he hadn't banked on. Things during Group Therapy, things inside him – frightening confusing raging things. It's Callum again. Talking publicly about how he was sexually abused as a teenager by one of the houseparents in care. He's going on and on about how he's come to terms with his past and how his experiences have taught him wisdom and compassion and ability to empathize.

The discussion moves on. Barry is saying how it all boils down to assertiveness and how he's grateful for the skills he's been taught at Chrysalis. The importance of assertiveness is really coming into its own, now that he's living a more independent existence. One day, and that could be any day now, someone out there's going to offer him a drink and he's got to have the strength to say no.

But that's just it, says Ronnie, no one's got the strength to stand up to anyone these days. Everything's going down the tubes. He respects it when the staff take a tough line. His father didn't tolerate any nonsense when he was alive and Ronnie respected that – he hated not knowing where he stood. His mum was too soft by half. She let him get away with murder after his dad died – she bought him sweets and toys and anything he wanted, but this was weakness. He despises weakness. If his mum had stood up to him when he was out of line, she'd have earned his respect a lot more. But that's all up the swannie too – good old-fashioned discipline. Everyone's too soft.

Jeff says that the staff try to strike a fine balance between firmness and kindness, and does anyone else have anything to say on the matter, especially any of the girls who have been unusually quiet today, and Faith says, you mean the women, and Shona says her parents can be their own worst enemy, actually, they can be too kind for their own good, just as Ronnie said, and although it's an awful thing to say, sometimes it was like her parents didn't want her to get better, because having a drug addict for a daughter gave them a weird sense of purpose and that's why they're dysfunctional. As a family. It brought them together, it was like a common interest they shared: the helping, the rushing about after her and defending her in court. Because before the drugs her parents didn't have that much to say to each other, and Vanessa, shades off, shakes her head and says addicts don't bring families together, they tear them apart.

Then it's time for coffee and tea and cigarettes, and people take their time because Group Therapy can be heavy-going.

And so the therapy sessions go on week by week, only now Michael feels more uptight and irritable than ever, and whenever he deals the cards in the coffee lounge, they overturn or skid off the table, much to the annoyance of his opponents, and sometimes – if he gets a bad hand – he'll claim that people have fiddled his cards. You twisting or sticking, Michael, they'll say, and he'll tell them to stick the game.

It's like speeding without speed, but they make allowances. It's all this heavy stuff he's doing with Faith. He's been up to the loft. An invisible handle's been turned at the side of his mind, sending all his memories – near and far, active and dormant, good and bad – into an uncontrollable spin.

So whenever he can, he disappears off to the relaxation room with its cool blue walls, or some quiet place in the woods to chill out with the dogs, to let the wasps settle down, and he'll take out his tin whistle and try out a tune.

7

On arrival for her interview at The Chrysalis Trust, the first thing Cheryl notices is how empty the house is. "Most of them have gone out to the New Forest today in the minibus," says Anthea Sparrow, the project manager, probably early fifties. During the interview, Anthea talks about the humanist ethos at Chrysalis, and how they cater for both men and women, both drug and alcohol problems, while Cheryl reminds herself of the further amendments to her identity. She is not only Cheryl West now, but this time she's decided not to mention her four children should anyone ask: it'll save her from those intrusive questions, like the kind Marcia asks at 484. She wants to put her old life behind her and be a full-time career woman.

After the interview, Anthea takes her on a tour around the rural house. "The women's rooms are on this floor. The men's above." After the house tour, Cheryl's shown around the grounds and the workshops, where one of the residents is making something on a pottery wheel. She's taken past chickens and goats and vegetable plots. "The smaller houses over here are the re-entry houses for residents later on in the programme, who live more independently. Yew Tree Lodge is the women's, and the one on your left, Oak Tree Lodge, is the men's." She meets one or two part-time staff, and a resident called Vanessa who makes her a cup of tea and doesn't take off her sunglasses once.

"How much notice do you need to give in your present job, Cheryl?"

"One calendar month."

Cheryl knows she's got the job, something in her bones, that nonverbal stuff you get, so it's no surprise when she gets first the phone call, then the official written offer of the job. She won't let it be a source of upheaval, she won't even have to move from Tea Rose Cottage necessarily, though she will need to get herself some decent wheels if she's going to be driving regularly to and from rural Hampshire, and now that she's leaving 484 she doesn't want to go. Last minute nerves, they tell her, and they'll miss her, but it's too good an opportunity to miss.

An opportunity. She tries not to lose sight of that word as she works her month's notice.

8

Faith considers the crucial stage of rehabilitation Michael has reached, and pleased with his progress, she walks along with him in the dappled light of the wooded area. He is mostly quiet, except to talk to Woodstock, scrabbling in the earth, but it's a different sort of quiet. In their counselling sessions he has opened up and – in spite of overwhelming predictions to the contrary – has given her permission to do the anonymous case study on him as part of her course assignment.

"We could do our session out here again today, Michael. Like we did the other day."

"Yeah," he says, hurling a stick for Woodstock to retrieve. "I can talk easier when we're outside."

"It's lovely out here, isn't it, now that summer's on the way."

"Yeah. I feel more relaxed out here."

"And you're still happy for me to tape our sessions?"

"Yeah. Did it record OK out here last time?"

"Yeah, it was pretty good quality," she says. "And don't forget, I'll always switch it off if you can't handle it, OK?"

"Yeah." They've come to a clearing in the woodland where some children are flying kites on the heathland. "What did you say you were doing with them again?"

"Transcribing notes. For my case study."

"Oh yeah." He falls quiet for a moment as he watches the children in the distance. The air is alive with the flap and whizz of nylon as the kites loop in the breeze. "I used to have a kite," he says. "Did I tell you?" He gets up and sits on the gate. "Mine was just a simple sort, like you see in kids books and that. Not like these high tech things." He then jumps down from the gate, leaning on it instead, still watching the kites. "I used to think my kite was a bird that never flew away."

*

With every week that passes, Faith sees further changes in Michael's behaviour. The flare-ups are fast dwindling, and he lets people hug him now, even hugs them in return. He's almost ready to start doing some voluntary work in the community and she's glad to have helped him this far. But she is always cautious. It's still a strain on him, on all of them, trying to be one of the clan. There's so much pressure to conform and participate, to be like the others. The long-term residents are the most guilty of applying the pressure. Burnt-out with years of living on the edge they cherish normality for themselves and everyone else.

And she should know …

But in quiet corners she picks up an undercurrent. An unsettled feeling in Michael…

9

Michael keeps his eyes on the chessboard. There's still this thing between him and Callum, this unspoken sexual thing, but they have to keep it under wraps. Callum's not that interested in the chess, he's interested in them spending time together, legit time, and chess gives him plenty of that because chess can take forever.

"You see," says Callum between moves, "it's taken me all my life to figure out this one, but other people aren't half as wrapped up in my past and my problems as I thought. They've got their own lives. Okay, so it's an awful thing being molested as a youngster but the whole world doesn't stop because of it. Life goes on."

Callum's talk is always one-way in chess. Michael likes to keep his mind on the game, which could still go either way; they've only taken a couple of pawns each, but things are hotting up. His own pieces are advancing, poised for attack, because he's got this knack of being able to concentrate on all angles at once – strategy and conversation – without appearing to do so. It foils the opposition. Lulls them into a false sense of advantage.

"And if anybody did show any interest," says Callum, tentatively fingering a bishop, "they were all voyeurs and sadists, as far as I was concerned. They had to be. They were getting some perverse pleasure from my pain which they called job satisfaction."

Michael takes Callum's bishop from its new square. It's been annoying him for ages, that blinking bishop: the one on the white diagonal. "Should have seen that coming," says Callum. "Anyway, I reckoned if they were that upset, I mean really upset, they wouldn't be able to do the job – it'd be too devastating, right?"

Callum's words might have strategy, but his defence is falling apart. Most of his pieces are sitting ducks, but he doesn't seem that bothered any more. "That's the way I thought when I first came here, but I don't think that way no more. Most of what they teach here is spot on."

Callum moves his king out of check from Michael's knight, the same knight which is about to nab his queen, though Callum's unfazed. "I've learnt here that doing your worksheets is as important as making your bed in the morning or cooking dinner for everyone or washing the loos."

There's no stopping the tide of check now – he's got Callum boxed in. All Callum can do is keep moving himself out of check until there's nowhere else to go.

One more move is all it'll take. And now Michael swoops his rook forward through a bare, undefended piece of board to perform the final kill, though Callum still thinks there's one safe square left for his king. "It can't go there," he says. "Can't go there coz of the pawn, there coz of that knight. That's it, isn't it?" he says, as he reaches across to shake Michael's hand. "Who taught you to play. anyway? Your pa, wasn't it?"

Michael nods.

"Well," says Callum, "he may have done you wrong, but he sure taught you a mean game of chess."

"He taught me lots."

Callum's still going on – it's all pouring out without a let-up. His biggest regret, he says, is leaving it too late with his own pa, because of being put in care by his ma and pa because they couldn't handle him, because he was out of control, and he bore them a grudge for years because of what happened to him there – the abuse and that. He tried to mend the rift with them several times, when he was a bit older, about nineteen or twenty, but they always rowed with him and sent him packing because of the drugs. They were worried about the effect on his wee brother but he couldn't see that because he was too wrapped up in his own selfish lifestyle, and so he cut them out of his life. Even when he heard that his pa had lung cancer he still had no compassion, that's how bad he'd become, he just remembered how his pa had slagged him off all those times for his self-inflicted drug use and there was his pa now lying in hospital full of tubes because he'd smoked himself there and so precious time was lost and by the time he decided to make the peace with his pa it was too late.

"I've regretted it ever since, Michael. Don't you do the same. Whatever your pa's done – make peace with him while you can."

He thinks about what Callum's just said. His dad may be dead, too, for all he knows. Seven years is a long time. Most of the other residents have some family contact. He's forced to put up with blow-by-blow accounts of weekend visits to relatives or even worse – parents and brothers and wives and daughters – coming here to Chrysalis. Between times, he tries to forget that other people still have families. But there always seems to be someone's relatives drifting about the place these days. Through the window, even now, there's Shona walking with her mother on the clean-shaven lawn, under trees bright lime with sunshine. Reunited after some long-standing feud.

"I'm gonna miss this place," says Callum as he packs the chessmen away and strokes the cat rubbing against his leg. "Only a couple of weeks to go now."

"Wish I was leaving."

"You're doing just fine, Michael. You hang on in there and complete your rehab and then you can come and live with me on the outside, yeah?"

Why hang on in there? He's ready now. He's worked on himself. He's drug-free. He's got all he can from Chrysalis. Stuff about dysfunctional families and empowerment and loving the inner child.

He's ready for the world.

10

For her first morning at Chrysalis, Cheryl decides to dress down. After agonizing over what to wear, buttoning and unbuttoning blouses and skirts, she finally opts for the smart casual look: loose navy blue trousers, hint-of-pink blouse, gold stud earrings. A bit softer round the tips than her usual office wear.

Now, as she sits in Anthea's office, she discovers that Anthea is an ex-teacher which may explain why she talks about the residents as though they're still at school. She keeps mentioning how "vunrable" some of them are, especially "the new boys and girls" though some of them look over forty.

"They've got so much stuff to deal with," says Anthea, in that slightly Welsh accent of hers. Stuff is clearly a euphemism for personal problems. Anthea is now discussing more immediate practicalities, like the personal possessions of staff members. "It's not fair on residents if temptation's put in their way," she explains, "so all handbags and what-not can be locked away in this drawer here." What a tactful way of putting it, Cheryl thinks. It's our fault for being unfair and not theirs for being light-fingered.

As she's escorted into the coffee lounge, she tries to imagine herself shopping or swimming or making pots with a bunch of delinquents. It's one thing interviewing them for surveys, quite another spending all day with them. "This is Cheryl," says Anthea by way of announcement at the entrance to the lounge, before being called away on some other business. Without hesitation, Cheryl walks over to a seat by the window and sits down.

When she's had a chance to get her bearings she takes a look around, though she isn't sure who are the residents and who, if any, the members of staff. She doesn't recognize anyone from the day of the interview. That big-breasted girl with the dirty blond hair and tattoo-covered arms, aiming cigarettes, like darts, at all the other smokers in the circle – she isn't staff, for sure.

"Here catch, Ronnie."

"Sokay, Shona. I'm back on rollies."

Shona's uncompromising gaze alights on Cheryl. "Ju smoke?"

"It's okay, I smoke these." Cheryl holds up her own like a pack of cards.

"Oh fuck." The room is deathly silent as Shona strikes two matches together in vain. "Gizza light, Ronnie," she says, and he chucks over her his throwaway lighter which she catches in one hand. She then shakes it up and down, lights up, tosses it back and turns on Radio One. "That's better," she says, jigging her arms to the rhythms. "Sounded like a morgue in here."

"Hi, I'm Jeff," someone says to Cheryl's left and she finds herself shaking hands with a mild-eyed, bearded man who, she discovers during their brief conversation, has a nursing background. Jeff then introduces her to Barry on his other side – a bloated red-faced hulk of man who unashamedly describes himself as a Recovering Alcoholic.

"Been back on the wagon three months," says Barry proudly. "I'm just taking it one day at a time."

This has her wondering – now that she's feeling relaxed enough to do a quick stock-take of everyone in the room – just who are (or were) the drinkers and who the drug addicts. The guy Ronnie with the gaunt face and grim teeth, the one back on rollies, he's definitely drugs, while over there is a lizard-face anorexic sitting in an armchair apart from the others, feet tucked under her, disengaged stare into the middle distance – oh yes, you can still see the purple heroin rings under her eyes.

Jeff says, "Ready for your video then, Heather?"

"Kerry can go before me," says Heather, with the long straight hair and bright smile. The sort of woman you can picture in church shaking a tambourine. "She's newer than me."

"Did mine this morning," says the Lizard Face, without moving a muscle.

"Wait till you look back on yourselves in three months time, girls," says Barry. "Talk about metamorphosis."

Cheryl turns to Jeff. "Video?"

"Oh it's an effective way of marking progress," he says. "All residents are video'd when they first arrive and then approximately every three months thereafter."

*

In the afternoon, Cheryl's just stroking one of the cats, a black and white one with a scratched nose, when she sees someone sprinting over to her. It's Lesley Sweet – her first ever guinea-pig for the 484 research. As well as gaining about two stone in weight, Lesley now has shorter, darker hair and is dressed in a tracksuit instead of the smart suits she was famous for.

"You didn't recognize me for a moment, did you?" Lesley slaps a leg. "Not with my thunder thighs. It's all the food we eat here."

That's it, yes. Lesley's put on so much weight, she almost looks pregnant.

"So they've sent you here now to do your surveys, have they?"

"No, I'm not doing that any more. I'm working here as a Rehab Assistant. This is my first day."

"Really? In that case, welcome aboard."

"So how long have you been here, Lesley?"

"Nearly a year now. I'm living over at Yew Tree Lodge – the women's re-entry house. Why don't you come back and have a coffee and I'll show you round."

They walk the several hundred yards from the main house to Yew Tree Lodge, the place where female residents lead more independent lives. Inside the house, it's all fresh and light, no cutting corners here, no scrimping on the paint, and while Lesley brews up she talks about her son who's being looked after by her mother at the moment. She talks about the A Level she's been studying and the voluntary work she's been doing up at the nursery – the plant sort, that is, not the baby sort. "It was Faith got me into that. Have you met Faith, the black lady, attractive? Right on the ball, she is."

"Would you like to see some of my worksheets while you're here? See the kind of stuff we do? Chrysalis is very much about the work we do on ourselves as we prepare to become butterflies – and that means a lot of delving into ourselves, though we're protected and cocooned while we do that work.

"What's this? Oh yes, that was *that* exercise. What I lose by giving up drugs versus what I gain by giving up drugs. Oh, look, money was on top of my gains list, so I wasn't that dopey, even when I was still quite new. There's a little calculation here, see? If I spend £100 a week on gear, say, in ten years' time I'll have saved over fifty grand. Wow!

"You can always make a positive from a negative. Instead of saying the sun's gone in, here we say the clouds are covering the sun, but the sun is still shining away somewhere behind. It's all there inside us, but many people can't get at it because they're too clogged up with years of muck that's been slung their way … bet you think I've gone all weird and deep, don't you?

"You see, unless we get rid of the muck and believe there's something behind it, we won't last here. Not many complete the programme, you know. But I'm nearly there. I want to go down in the archives as one of those who made it."

"See over there?" she says, pointing through the window at another building nestling at the edge of the woods. "That's the old school house which is going to be the new family unit when they've finished converting it. It'll mean that mothers – and fathers – won't have to be separated from their children while they do rehab."

*

"Apart from Kerry and Heather, the other residents have all been here some time," Anthea explains to Cheryl at the staff meeting. "It's not good to have too many new people at once, until the others have had a chance to settle in."

Faith nods, with a swish of her long black dreadlocks. "Imagine if Kerry had come to a chaotic house. She'd have certainly left by now."

"Lesley was saying that not many make it to the end of the programme," says Cheryl.

"No," says Anthea. "Callum was our most recent 'graduate'. He left a fortnight ago and took one of our other residents with him."

"But even a few months benefited Michael enormously," says Faith.

"Yes," says Anthea, while Cheryl reflects on how much there is to take in. It's a different world to 484.

But in a matter of weeks, she is soon familiar with the schedule of activities that form the structure at Chrysalis. There are the daily ones, like driving to the shops and cleaning and meal preparation, there are the twice weekly ones, like group therapy and counselling, and the weekly ones like the house meetings and staff meetings and the visit to the library and the visit from the psychiatrist, Dr Body. There are the other optional activities each week as well, like swimming, yoga, Tai Chi, meditation, gardening, art.

Now, here she is in the coffee lounge as she is every morning, only now she's a known face. "You know you're on cleaning duties this morning," she reminds Shona. Shona's been a bit of a tough nut to crack, but just lately she's started to yield. You might not think so to look at her now, mind you, sitting there, throwing chewing-gums at everyone in turn, ignoring the comment. It's a battle of wills, a battle which Shona will certainly lose, because duties have to be done, but it doesn't stop Shona holding out as long as is respectfully possible or using every diversionary tactic in the book. It makes Cheryl think just how like children they are.

"Oi Barry," Shona shouts. "You sound merry! Go out last night, did you?"

"Like a light," he says, and then looks at Cheryl. "I hope she's not giving you a hard time."

"Course I'm not." Shona retaliates by hitting Barry playfully on the arm. "I was just going to show her my room before getting stuck into the bathrooms, wasn't I, Cheryl?"

This is a real breakthrough, because Shona's is the only bedroom in the main house Cheryl's not yet seen and she's surprised to find a posse of fluffy animals on her quilt cover. She might have expected to find them in Lesley's room, or Kerry's – (though Kerry's is quite bare, her personality not yet ready for self-expression) – but not Shona's.

Between the Stone Roses posters sellotaped to the wardrobe, she finds herself drawn to a silkscreen print of a wild-haired woman on a motorbike.

"That's my favourite," says Shona. "Got loads. D'you want one? I've got different coloured ones.   Black-and-red.   Blue-and-red. Brown-and-white."

"I like the red-and-blue."

"Makes your eyes go all weird, that one. You can have it."

"Cheers."

"I know they say giving away your art is a bit like giving away your baby. I know all about that an' all. I haven't seen my Chelsea since she was a babbee. Had to have her adopted."

Oh, tell me about it, Cheryl thinks. The adoption option. That was Diana's suggestion when Cheryl told her she was pregnant again for the fifth time. But she couldn't go through with all that again, not at her time of life. The pains in the legs, the back, the constant weeing, the haemorrhoids. No way. She imagined it getting fatter and fatter, like a tumour wrapping itself around her vital organs and crushing her breath away, as she ached and staggered and groaned. No no. She imagined her hands never feeling clean from wiping a dirty bum all day, and she would wrestle with her pre-packaged dinners in their cellophane, fish in parsley sauce, one for her, one for Luigi, one for Juliet, and she would slit the plastic of each one, give it a squeeze, and out it would come, thudding down like a constipated foetus, all the messy sauce seeping out behind.

Life had become just as humdrum with Luigi, after all. She didn't want to be part of a convoy of pushchairs, holding up the pedestrians along the narrow pavement. Nor to wear that distracted-mother look – in one ear, out the other – when people tell you things of the utmost importance. Nor to accrue half-watched films or half-read books, all abandoned for the sake of a full nappy or a bruised knee or a new tune on some stupid toy piano. Yet there she was, sorting out the clothes in the airing cupboard ready for ironing, or watering the plants – filler chores that you could just about squeeze in when you had the odd ten minutes to spare, and you only ever had minutes, like some only ever had pennies. If your resources are scarce, you squander them because you can't do anything with them.

She remembers she was sitting at the kitchen table – still uncleared from breakfast – when she told Diana she was pregnant again.

"Great!" Diana's expression then backtracked. "Or is it?"

"I'll be forty-three next birthday." Cheryl watched her Alka-Seltzer fizz into oblivion. "What do you think?"

"Well...that's not old these days."

"I feel run ragged. I want a life."

"Well...if you really don't want it ...there's always the adoption option. What does Luigi say?"

"He doesn't know yet. God, my womb feels like a lodging house." She knew she wouldn't have to elaborate, not to Diana who wrote the Viola journal. But that's what it was like. It was like letting a room for nine months at a time, and a lot of hard work when it came to eviction because the lodgers never wanted to leave, but there comes a time to finish the letting, because the room gets too worn and torn, the landlady too weary.

"What should I do, Di?"

"Don't you think you should discuss it with Luigi?"

"It's my body."

"OK. We can go through the options ... but it's got to be your choice in the end, Cheryl."

Options? Choices? But she wanted Diana to play mother. Do this, do that. Orders. That's what she wanted. She'd been in charge of all her men, but who would look out for her? Suddenly she wanted someone to make her hot cereal on cold mornings and tell her to dress up warm. Children got it all done for them and they didn't even want it, and they certainly didn't appreciate it, the ungrateful gits. Give it to us, adults! But Diana wasn't going to decide for her. It's got to be your choice, Cheryl. Diana was harping on about options and responsibilities but where on earth did she learn such junk? Diana of all people. God, those words stuck in the throat, along with commitments and husband and children. But she didn't want to be child-centred any more. There was another: child-centred! The one all the experts said was the key to successful parenting. Well, Successful Parenting be buggered.

She wanted to be a Successful Woman. She wanted those little luxuries back: a few days in bed when you're ill, with lemon barley and a box of tissues and food brought to you on a tray, or buying yourself a new pair of shoes, or selfishly pursuing that dream where you sing your heart out in a smoky cellar with Peter de Cruz ...

Or a career.

She didn't want to be seduced into forgetting the pain of childbirth, or join the conspiracy that keeps the pain private. This time she wanted to remember, to hang onto the memory because she didn't want to let her room any more. She wanted to put up the closed sign. To be unpregnant.

And then it hit home, a couple of days after her termination. There was demolition work everywhere – the whole of Bournemouth was being mown down or dug up, it seemed. Empty houses toppled while she stayed standing. Too bad. It was time they went. Houses had boxed her in enough. They'd prefixed and defined and confined her. Housewife. Housework. Housebound.

But at last she was uninhabited. No room to let, and all the boards up.

She went to the beach, which had its end-of-the-season look. Wasps hanging vertically and being blown off course, like the seagulls. Deckchairs chained in a stack against the lamp-posts. Air fresh and schooly. That time of year when you have your last serious stab at sunbathing, before you soak in your autumn baths, rubbing off your tan with the balls of your fingers. But she had made her decision. It was just a matter of executing it.

And then, a few months after, she left Juliet and Luigi behind and re-potted herself back in London.

It was time to be someone else, somewhere else.

11

At the team meeting, most of the staff are still recovering from the grave news concerning one of their former residents, Callum, who, it has been disclosed, recently died of an overdose. Though Cheryl herself didn't know him, there are a lot of shock waves coming from the people who did, and a long discussion ensues about improving aftercare.

Once the stunned feelings have subsided, they go on to discuss Shona, discharged yesterday. They discuss her discharge at some length. "She brought drugs into the house," Faith explains for the benefit of the newest volunteer, Peggy, who – Cheryl thinks – has a very stupid kind of face. She looks like a Peggy, in fact, with her pinned-together nostrils, as though she really does have a peg on her nose. Peggy responded to an appeal for volunteers in the local press, and looks like a do-gooder sort. "Oh, I thought she seemed a little dreamy," says Peggy, "when we were playing that game yesterday. She said she felt as if she was floating through the day. It was my suggestion, you know, to think of words ending in 'dom'. I started off with freedom and then Heather said Christendom and someone else said stardom and then Shona said con– " Anthea looks at her watch. "Thank you, Peggy." Anthea says they all need to try and put both incidents behind them: Callum's tragic death and Shona's discharge. It's important the community looks forward, she says, and starts discussing the Willows, the new family house which has recently opened its doors to its first family: Alan and Dorothy and their daughter. Anthea also stresses other positive changes to boost the morale of her team: Barry's voluntary work (clearing ponds and paths), and Lesley soon to be moving into her new lodgings with her son, where she'll be able to complete her studies and get some more valuable work experience in the wider community.

Cheryl drifts off. She realizes she's gasping for a cigarette – the meeting has already overrun by fifteen minutes – and she's tired because she's just moved to Winchester. Janet, the dentist's widow, finally returned from her travels to Tea Rose Cottage, (though Diana's now backpacking in Australia. Good old Diana, a kindred spirit, having broken free from the old life). Janet came up with an alternative living arrangement for Cheryl. "I've got this homeopath friend, a Mrs Howard," she said. "Part of her house is converted into flatlets which she rents out to friends, or friends of friends. It's in Winchester. That would be ideal for you, wouldn't it?"

*

And when Cheryl gets home, clouds have moved in from the west.

Elaine. Crouched on the outer steps of Mrs Howard's home, surrounded by a ring of cigarette butts, and looking ever more brutal with her black hair and eyeliner and sour-cream face. And her clothes have that shut-in-a-drawer smell.

As Cheryl opens the front door, she senses something open-ended about this visit. Maybe it's to do with the size of Elaine's luggage.

"I need to be away from that town," says Elaine, following Cheryl upstairs. "Hey, this is better than that awful twee bungalow. More character."

"And less room." Cheryl unlocks her own front door. "It's what you call a flatlet."

"I don't care what it's called. I'll crash anywhere. I don't mind."

"I mind. You can see how pushed I am for space." She hands Elaine a dustpan and brush. "And before you get too settled, you can sweep up those fag ends. It doesn't exactly create a healthy impression for Mrs Howard's clients now, does it?"

"Clients? Oh yeah, I saw the doctor's plaque outside."

"Mrs Howard is a homeopath. She has her surgery on the ground floor."

"Does she have any other flats going begging?"

"No. The other flat's taken. Anyway, you've got a flat in Bournemouth."

Elaine doesn't answer, but switches on the TV and sits in the armchair with her legs dangling over one side, looking so nonchalant and brattish as she agitates that bottle of Mary Quant nail varnish, until it comes up all pretty and two-tone, like navy blue silk. It's all rich and smooth as it coats her nails, because it hasn't got to that grainy stage where all it's fit for is the potatoes in your tights. She then waves her nails in the air to dry, giving them a little blow every so often.

When she's sure they're dry, no sign of stickiness, she unzips a pocket in her holdall and pulls out some photographs. "I came across these the other day, when I was at dad's."

"How is your dad?"

"You might find out yourself if you ever contacted him."

"Why would I want to do that? Anyway, he's got his new house and new woman and everything, hasn't he? Whatshername, Jane."

"Mum, the house is hardly new…he's been in it a year."

Cheryl harrumphs. "So…are you going to show me these photos then?"

Elaine passes them across and Cheryl sorts through them in silence. They look as angels, Elaine, Michael and Stephen, all still and captivating, like a flower arrangement, but they're out of context, they've never been like that. No kids ever have. They don't contain this much sugar. They spring leaks on your best chair and pick their noses and blub with a mouthful of biscuity mush.

"Well? They're good, aren't they?"

"Very nice."

"Liar."

"No, they are."

"What do you care? You don't even bother with *Stephen* any more."

"That's total crap. He's busy up there in Manchester, I'm busy down here. We keep in touch when we can." Though that's all they do. There's no quality to their talk these days, nor quantity. They don't have time to rub two sentences together in their busy-busy lives. Instead, their sentences remain half-strung together or hanging in the air, unfinished.

"And what about Michael? No word for nearly eight years. What does that say, eh?"

"How can I get in touch with him if I don't know where he is?"

"I never did get why he suddenly left home like that and not a squeak since. Mind you, I'm not surprised, the way you always treated him." Elaine gets up from the armchair. "You know, you're a right cold bitch sometimes," she says, and goes out to use the pay phone on the landing. She sits, back up against the bannister, and there's a lot of intense mumbling as she stretches and twiddles the coil of flex. When she comes off the phone, Cheryl asks who she was phoning, more for something to say than anything, and gets the full brunt of Elaine's tinderbox temper. "My life's got fuck all to do with you, who I phone, what I do, who I go out with," and then she swipes hold of her bag and swirls off back to Bournemouth in a cloud of melodrama.

By contrast, the weeks pass by more peaceably at work. Yes, there are minor, even major eruptions at Chrysalis, but it's all in a day's work.

And there are always new things to learn.

Anthea stops her one day, one of those rare, quiet days, and says, "I realize you've been with us a few months already, Cheryl, and we haven't given you any time off to go on any training courses. But we've plenty of training videos here. How about watching some of them this afternoon? It's quiet and you won't be disturbed."

So here she is on her own, drinking her coffee, having set up the video in the coffee lounge. She thought it'd be interesting, first off, to view some of the residents' videos. She'd like to see what Lesley looked like when she first arrived here, Barry and Ronnie too. She sorts through some videos and slots one in. Oh yes, there's Shona, looking pretty rough and sallow. She watches it for ten minutes or so, the black and white picture's not all that good, neither is the sound, and then she fast forwards to a young man with dreadlocks, sitting with head bowed, a black dog at his feet. Both he and the dog seem to have a slight tremor all over, or maybe it's just the picture, and then the camera zooms in close, and she cups her hands over her face.

It can't be.

It *can't*.

"Turn that fuckin cam–," he shouts, and then there's the knocking of microphones and a lot of camera shake and finally a new piece of film. Kerry. She quickly checks the label on the video case which says, INDUCTIONS: SHONA, MICHAEL, KERRY. Then she hears someone outside the door, and quickly ejects the tape.

"Is it all working OK?" says Anthea. "Only we had a spot of bother with it last time."

Cheryl tries to look composed.

"Is everything all right, Cheryl? You're looking a bit– "

"Actually, I'm not feeling too good … I think I'm going to have to go home and lie down."

12

At home, Elaine is back again and gradually getting her feet under the table, so she can move her boyfriend in when the time is right, Cheryl supposes. Not in this flatlet – even Elaine isn't stupid enough to think that three people could share such a tiny space – but she's been carefully working on Mrs Howard for that room across the landing, the one she knows is soon to be vacant. Mrs Howard, out most evenings at this or that lecture or course or play, is easily charmed. Mrs Howard doesn't see or hear the dark side of Elaine, the one who scowls about the house. No, she says it gives her great faith in the Youth of Today when she meets a nice youngster like Elaine.

But Mrs Howard will notice soon, surely. She'll notice how Elaine's started to look more slovenly, behind her make-up and pseudo-smart appearance. She'll notice that Elaine only needs to sleep in the sheets once for them to look dirty, that her inside collars all have a line of grime. It's something Cheryl can't understand, not when she's so meticulous about such matters. In other areas though, Elaine is scrupulous. Each morning she sits cross-legged on the floor, mirror in hand, inside a ring of pretty-coloured cotton wool balls and face-creams and lotions. She's obsessed with her face, even to the point of looking at her reflection in such unlikely places as kitchen knives and fish slices.

It makes Cheryl feel claustrophobic. As though she's still fighting for her autonomy; her right to be what she wants without admonishment from her daughter. But Elaine's presence is a constant reminder of where she went wrong. Maybe she's just more aware of all the little annoying things because she's taken a few days sick leave to collect her thoughts. She's decided not to tell Elaine about Michael. She has visions of the two of them getting together and ganging up on her. Neither can she tell anyone at Chrysalis; they know her only as a career woman called Cheryl West, children never mentioned. She could just leave, she supposes, but she needs the resources of Chrysalis to piece together the missing years, to give her some answers, to put her on the trail.

So she returns to work, feeling more composed, and with a plan ready to put into action. She knows there are files on all the residents, past and present, but the only people with access are the senior workers who, she imagines, guard them with their lives as they do their own diaries. She knows, too, that the secretarial cover has been basic and transient, and that Anthea is keen to update and expand the database, though it's never been done in a methodical fashion to date. And so Cheryl volunteers her services: she has the research skills and computer expertise from 484, she says, and Anthea is, of course, delighted. She has even arranged a volunteer to cover Cheryl's other duties for half a day a week, until the job is done. "This is important work, Cheryl," she says. "I appreciate just how long information-gathering and data entry can take. But we urgently need to tighten up on our computerized records. Funding can depend on it."

Cheryl has created the opportunity, a perfectly legitimate one, to browse through the files at leisure, while ostensibly searching for information to enter on the database.

But now she's sitting here in the quiet back office, tucked away and cut off from the hubbub of the front office, she feels apprehensive. She can't make a bee-line for the file she wants, she has to work up to it gradually, and she does this by finding her way round some other neutral files first, gathering and collating the information she needs. Things like substance use, age of first use, agency of referral, and other demographic details. She goes to the filing cabinet and pulls out several files with names she recognizes. Wayne Ronald Costello (must be Ronnie) dob 29.1.62 (she'd have put him older than twenty-nine.) Alan Robert Stanley Granville dob 19.11.53. Dorothy Anne Granville dob 26.2.52. Shona Louise Keen dob 30.11.65.

Michael John Pullen dob 14.5.67.

She takes the files to the table and puts Michael's on top. She stares at it, desperate to read it, afraid to. What if someone should interrupt her? She reminds herself that she's not doing anything surreptitious by opening it: she's got a job to do, one that Anthea's asked her to do, and she has to read through them all to obtain the necessary information.

She opens the file and finds what look like pages of selected transcripts from an interview or something – all perfectly typed up and stapled together in the pocket at the front of the file. This is the real dilemma. She doesn't need to read this. All the demographic details can probably be found fairly easily from the various pink and green forms, somewhere at the back of the file, but she's just got a glimpse of one of the later transcripts, though she can't make head or tail of it. Something about a hostel.

M – I call it Hell Hostel.

F – Why was that?

M – There were these people there – therapists and healers they said. They shone lamps in my face and put stuff in my drinks that made me sleepy. They could mind-read.

F – How do you mean?

M – They knew stuff about me. Perhaps they couldn't mind-read. I might have blurted it all out when they spiked my drinks. They kept talking to me about therapy and making these comments.

F – What sort of comments?

M – Like – Are-you-feeling-below-'pa' today? Pa without the R. I-should-put-it-behind-you. That was another.

F – What was this 'therapy'?

M – They had me doing these role-plays with them. They said it was therapy. To help me, they said. They played the bad guys and they filmed it all, and then we had to watch the film afterwards.

F – No wonder you didn't want to do the video when you first arrived.

M – They would stop and replay bits where I was being too passive or too angry and that.

F – And was there any physical contact during these role plays?

M – Yeah.

F – What physical? Sexual?

M – Everything.

Cheryl shakes her head, stunned, but is unable to digest the full import of it because Anthea has just come through to the back office. She quickly stuffs the file back in the pile on the desk. She picks out another at random – Barry's as it happens – and pretends to be going through it with a fine toothcomb for that important information. Silly really, when she thinks about it – as if Anthea could give a toss which file she's looking at, as if Anthea's got the time or inclination. Anthea's only interest is the computer. Is it working all right? Cheryl says she thinks it is though she won't know for sure until she starts inputting the data, which won't be for a while yet. Sure, sure, says Anthea.

Anthea finishes her buzzing about and when she's gone, Cheryl retrieves Michael's file. She opens it at the beginning of another transcript and sees the word 'mother'.

F – We talked a little in the last session about your positive memories of your mother. Now I'm going to ask if you have any negative memories of her.

M – Plenty.

F – Any examples?

M – When she'd been drinking.

F – Can you remember anything specific?

M – She was always criticizing me and telling me I was stupid.

F – For example?

M – You're always dropping things and breaking things she'd say, like if I tried to make her a cup of tea or something. I could never do it right.

F – Is that why you didn't like being on teas and coffees?

M – Maybe. Oh and I would get these bad asthma attacks as a kid but she never took it seriously like my dad did, even when I was, like, in danger.

F – Why do you think that was?

M – She thought it was all, like, psychological and that I was putting it on, I suppose.

F – So she wouldn't always respond in an emergency?

M – She probably done it teach me a lesson.

F – Why should she do that?

M – Coz I was a nuisance to her being ill all the time, I suppose, or maybe she thought it would make me snap out of it, I dunno.

F – Do you feel you were emotionally abused by her?

M – Dunno.

F – From what you're saying it sounds like she constantly undermined you. Would that be a fair thing to say?

M – I suppose so.

F – Why would she do that, do you think?

M – Dunno. Any ideas?

F – Maybe she was jealous of the closeness between you and your father.

M – Maybe.

F – Perhaps she wanted to be close to you, but felt pushed out by your closeness to your dad, so she took it out on you.

M – D'you reckon?

F – What do you reckon?

M – I dunno. I can't get my head round all that scheming stuff.

F – Did she ever hit you?

M – Sometimes.

F - What would she hit you for?

M – The usual things I suppose. I don't remember.

F – You don't remember any specific occasions.

M – When I wet the bed.

F – Was that once? More than once?

M – More than once yeah and then she'd make me change the fucking sheets and wash them.

F – How old would you have been at this time?

M – About nine.

F – You were about nine, and were you experiencing any emotional upset or trauma at that time which caused you to wet the bed?

(I switched the tape off at this point because M broke down and eventually disclosed about the Child Sex Abuse – F)

F – Do you remember when the abuse first started?

M – I'm not sure. It's all a bit of a blur. I think it was after we'd gone fishing one time.

F – Take your time.

M – I remember I got cold and we went back to this little house, like a lodge or something, dunno whose it was but there was this, like, log fire...I was sitting up close to him with a towel round me...I thought at first he was just towelling me dry...

F – You don't have to tell me anything you don't want to. I'm not interested in the details – only your feelings about it.

M – I just feel like I'm betraying him.

F – You feel protective of him, don't you?

M – Well, I don't want you just to see him like that. They all get tarred with the same brush, don't they?

F – Who abusers?

M – See what I mean? He may be an abuser to you, but he's my dad.

Andrew! No! Well, she's heard it all now. First her, now Andrew. How could he do it? How could he say such evil things? Maybe they believe all their filthy lies, after a while. But it's all rubbish. Complete and utter rubbish. Worse. It's slander. It's all too easy these days, to claim you've been abused. There was none of this nonsense in her day.

She closes her eyes, she doesn't want to recollect... she'd got herself a key to that flat Andrew minded for his friend. She was suspicious of him spending all that time at the flat. She crept in, she'd been waiting to catch Andrew with a woman and – bingo – on this occasion she thought she'd caught him. She heard sighs and grunts. When she sprung into the room, she saw two figures on the bed. But it was only Andrew and Michael. Andrew securing his flies. Both of them looking furtive. She said: What the hell...what's *he* doing here? It all happened so fast. She was too intent on looking for the woman. She looked in the wardrobe. Michael bolted. She shouted at Andrew. You disgust me! Where is she? Where's she hiding? And what was *he* doing here? Andrew blocked her way out of the room. OK, OK. There was a woman, but she was only showing Michael the ropes, Andrew said. It was just a rite of passage. Something to help Michael in that department, him being shy and all that.

She tried to calm down, even though she thought Andrew was lying. She thought both he and Michael had been at it with this girl, who had somehow made good her exit while Andrew was remonstrating with her.

F – What if we start today with some positive memories of your father?

M – We used to fly kites or go out in the boat ... it went on in the fuckin' boat as well, mind.

F – So the trips on the boat were positive in some respects and negative in others.

M – A lot of it was positive, I suppose. We'd spend the whole weekend on the boat sometimes and he'd let me have some booze.

F – And that felt good?

M – Yeah. I was only ten or eleven, so I felt grown up kind of thing.

F – Did you get drunk?

M – A bit tipsy. He drank most of it.

F – Did that make it easier for him to take advantage of you – the fact that you'd both had alcohol?

M – It played a part, I suppose.

F – So how do you feel on the whole about your weekends on the boat?

M – I liked the feeling of freedom on the water.

F – So on the whole you felt positive about these outings?

M – I just try and think of the good times and blank out the rest.

F – Do you have any other positive memories of your father?

M – He let me bunk off school. I hated school, as it goes. He taught me stuff at home. Cards and chess and that. Yeah and he taught me to drive when I was about twelve.

F – That must have been handy.

M – Yeah I loved it.

F – So apart from the abuse I'm getting the feeling you had a good relationship with him.

M – Yeah.

F – So when did the abuse stop?

M – See, I don't like that word. It wasn't real abuse what he did – not like you read in the papers and that. He wasn't violent or nothing. He never had to force me.

F – So what would you call it then?

M – Just a game.

F – And how did you feel about these 'games'?

M – Guilty.

F – Why was that?

M – It was wrong, wasn't it? Enjoying games like that.

F – It's not a crime to enjoy affection.

M – With your dad it is.

F – So when did it stop?

M – When I left home.

F – And when was that?

M – When I was sixteen.

F – So it was going on continuously for seven years?

M – No. Sometimes nothing would happen for weeks or months. Like in the school holidays and that. Although sometimes he took me to the flat he minded for a mate of his. You know, just to hang out.

F – But on the whole would it be right to say it happened more during term-time?

M – Yeah, I suppose it did.

F – You mean you didn't always go into school.

M – No. Sometimes my dad was home during the day if he was working nights.

F – So you had no real sanctuary either at school or home.

M – School was worse.

F – Worse than the abuse at home?

M – Yeah, because that'd be over in half an hour, if it happened at all whereas school went on all day. With no let up. You can't

escape bullies.. Sometimes I started out for school and then I'd come
home again. My dad knew I didn't like school, so he didn't make me
go.

F — So you must have got behind with your school work?

M — Yeah but like I said my dad taught me stuff at home. He told
me the best way to learn is to find something you want to know the
answer to and then work how it's done.

F — So when you did attend school did you feel out of step with
your peers?

M — Yeah. So I'd bunk off again. My dad was always writing me
sick notes. Half the time I was ill with my asthma anyway so I'd just
drag it out.

F – So when you stayed off school it was just you and your father
at home?

M – Yeah, my mother was at work, E was at school, S was away
at school.

F – And your mother didn't suspect anything?

M – Not as far as I know. Not until–

F – Not until?

M – She caught us…I hid in the bathroom…my dad tried to make
out there'd been a prostitute with us...but while they were arguing the
toss I shot off back home, packed a bag and left. I never went back.

No! She didn't believe it then and she doesn't believe it now! It's
all drug-addled lies! She believed Andrew's version. That was bad
enough, the idea of them with a prostitute but not this horrid
disgusting lies.   Perhaps he thinks there's money in it. Some
compensation or something – money is what they're all after, isn't
it?

F – What about E and S? Did they suspect anything?

M – I don't think so.

F – Did he abuse any of them to your knowledge?

M – Never talked to them about it. He spent more time with me.
He was closest to me.

F – What about your parents' relationship with each other?

M – What about it?

F – Did it seem satisfactory?

M – Not really.

F – Why was that?

M – She put him down all the time like she done me.

F – And how did he react to that?

M – He took no notice.

F – Did she deny him physical affection, do you think?

M – She did as it goes.

F – Is that what he told you?

M – Yeah. He said she didn't love him like a wife should and that she was always on the look-out for other men. He said Mr Ray needed affection and I could help Mr Ray.

F – Mr Ray?

M – Sounds sick, dunnit? But it was just a game like I said.

Cheryl looks up to find Dr Body, the psychiatrist, walking outside in the yard with Ronnie and Ronnie's ex who's here on a visit to see if there's any chance of her and Ronnie making a fresh go of things. Ronnie's ex is looking at Ronnie and Ronnie's looking down at his shoes and Cheryl feels a clammy feeling in her stomach, as if she's gorged down a lot of disgusting food and can't bear to eat another morsel.

Not the pink mist, but the red. The red mist is all around, fogging her vision.

She gets up and staggers to the relaxation room, wanting to puke it all out, and then she lies down, remembering the days, her singing-the-blues days, when her head spun with drink.

When she opens her eyes, Faith is standing there with a glass of water. "I think you overdid at the computer, Cheryl."

13

Juliet skips along the beach, ahead, and provides the small flurries of conversation between the long silences of her parents. "Here's a feather for you, mummy," she will say, through her new tombstone teeth. "Now I'll find one for you, daddy."

Luigi, now working in the beach cafeteria from March to the end of October, has filled out and greyed at the gills, making it hard for her to remember what the attraction was. She tries to imagine them as they were eight years ago, enjoying the shapes of their different bodies, hands, bottoms. Feeling the shapes, sharing the water and the sun.

It was an extravagant summer, like the child it created. That's Juliet. Extravagant in the extreme. Can I open the new blackcurrant juice? I want a new pair of shoes, mummy. These are all scratched. They're not new any more…

Not new any more. The words that always resonate. Oh no, not that again…

She squats down to Juliet's height, brushing the strands of hair from her eyes, but they blow back in again. Juliet looks honest enough, now, but there may be lies already in the making, lies that will set and harden with each passing year.

*

When Cheryl returns to Winchester, after her few days break in Bournemouth, she finds Elaine and her boyfriend, Matt, have moved into the flat across the landing, as predicted. She hears them as they indulge in late nights and fast food and tacky videos. They don't surface until after midday and when they do they hog and clog and fog the bathroom, though it seems to have miraculously escaped the notice of the health-conscious Mrs Howard, and Cheryl pictures another bathroom in Tooting where Elaine sat on the toilet, holding on to the seat, her pants around her ankles and her little legs straight out in front of her. One slip and she could have fallen down the bowl. She remembers that fear. She remembers the words, still misshapen, but beginning to make themselves understood. Wee-wees, ice gems, want to watch delly, and she falls into dreams about the time before words: the time of pattern and colour, the pink mist of birth. Elaine holding up a stick of green crayon and saying, Wednesday is green.

But Elaine is fully grown as she's saying it, with black hair and cigarettes, but she isn't Elaine at all, she's Michael, as he is on video, but when he opens his mouth he's got no teeth. Cheryl goes over to the pillow, which isn't a pillow at all, it's a tied up nappy, and underneath there's a tooth, teeth, a whole string, looking like milk teeth but she takes them into her hand and they become false teeth, plaster-cast dentures, like the kind you see in dental laboratories.

She wakes up, shuddering, and returns to work where she has to keep her secret well guarded, like a forbidden pregnancy, taking great pains to make sure it doesn't show. Maybe she could have told Faith, after the video, but not now, after the files. Now is too late. Faith will already have that mother earmarked as a gorgon.

And so, as the weeks pass, she tries to perform a sort of mental abortion. She's had one done before, after all, in the flesh. She imagines her secret being sucked out or broken up, never to grow or see or hear, and she finds, for a while, that it's not so difficult to lose herself in the other people and things happening at work. For one thing, there have been many changes. Many of the originals as she tends to think of them – Barry and Vanessa and Ronnie and Kerry – have all flown off to become butterflies, ready or not, and in their place there's been this latest influx of mature, stable characters – the heroin housewives, she calls them – who, Anthea says, will be good for the house, and television crews come to film life at Chrysalis and training videos have been made about Chrysalis for other workers in the field.

Then Lesley Sweet – that most perfect of Chrysalis butterflies – returns as a volunteer, having convinced staff that she is ready to follow her natural calling to help other addicts and alcoholics on the road to recovery. But for some reason the residents don't seem enamoured of Lesley. Something indefinable hovers about them. They seem suspicious of her and mistrustful of her success. Maybe they're jealous. Because she's made it and they haven't, and may never.

On the night of Lesley's birthday party, the women all go overboard with their frocks and blusher and earrings – any excuse to get dolled up – while the men stand in an awkward line at the buffet table, unsure whether to drool at the women, the food, or neither. Jeff is just dishing out the non-alcoholic punch from the huge ladle, when Lesley makes her grand entrance in a shoulderless dress, methadone-green in colour, with matching hair ribbon. She looks pathologically glamorous, like a drag queen, and the whispers grow. "It's not on," says one Heroin Housewife to another. "Can't they see her eyes?

She's pinned again. Totally off her face." The other Heroin Housewife frowns and says, "Yes, but she's their darling blue-eyed girl, isn't she? They don't want to see." But Lesley's eyelids are already drooping as the fruity tide in her glass turns choppy, and Cheryl knows this feeling, she knows what it's like to have everyone stare at you, putting pressure on you to perform, to sing, to sing Billie Holiday like you used to, and then Lesley sways into Arnie, one of the newer residents, christening his cream trousers a darker shade of cranberry. "Oh sorry, Arnie," her voice is slow, gouchy. "But we women get blood on our clothes all the time."

Arnie smiles and blushes and this has sealed Lesley's fate. She is quietly bundled off with names and numbers of people who can help mend her butterfly wings, and Cheryl goes home to the glug-glug of wine, or anything else that's handy, and raises a glass. Sweet Lesley, I salute you.

Then, one drink-rimmed evening, she thinks: Where are all the men these days? I still look sexy, don't I, in my pink satin slip with the thin straps, classy, like something Mrs Robinson might wear. Her from The Graduate. Or was hers black? Now *there* was a good role model for the more mature woman.

Mr de Cruz, she thinks. Why don't I give old Peter a ring?

She starts hunting for his number and when she's found it, she waits for Elaine to finish cradling the phone on the landing.

"How many have you had?" says Elaine, before disappearing into the smog of her room.

It's been years since she spoke to Peter, but when you're drunk, you're drunk. You just do things. That's all she wants to do, just talk, for old time's sake. She has first to get past the little girlfriend, of course, who sounds younger than Elaine. Peter must be, what, sixty? Easily by now, but she sees the tan-suede of his skin forming on the other end as he speaks. "Cheryl! So what's new?" She can still hear the croon in his voice, the crackle. They chat about their lives for a while and then he says, "Still drinking too much then, girl?"

"Listen. I may have a couple now and then– "

"You were a one," he says. "Such a temper on you when you'd had a few."

She doesn't want to continue with this. It wasn't why she phoned him. "Anyway, got to be going now, Peter," she says, and hangs up. She goes back to her room and wonders about phoning Andrew. Then she falls asleep.

14

Later in the summer, Faith drives over to Southampton in order to interview Michael, having finally tracked him down. It's part of the Chrysalis ethos, keeping tabs on former residents through their aftercare service, though some of them slip through the net. It was Cheryl's idea to do the follow-up research, after that faux pas with Lesley. Anthea was still trying to fathom out what went wrong with Lesley, when Cheryl said, "Perhaps we need to do more rigorous follow ups of former residents, Anthea. To find out what their weak points are, you know, once they're back in the community."

With her elbows on the table, Anthea thought for a while, sucking on her interleaved fingers. "You are absolutely right, Cheryl. There's been so little in the way of good follow-up research and yet it's so vital. Maybe we could have prevented Lesley's relapse if we'd known her vulnerable areas."

"And there was one of your other residents, the one who died, wasn't there?"

"You mean Callum. Yes. We've been forced to cutback on our aftercare service, but perhaps we need to be putting more resources into Relapse Prevention, and the research would certainly be one way."

"I've got the research skills," said Cheryl. "So if you wanted me to– "

"Well, maybe you and Faith could do it between you."

Something was subsequently cobbled together, while Anthea sorted out some cover and remuneration, and off Cheryl went to interview a few ex-residents, those easiest to track down, those most co-operative.

But Faith has been more than a little concerned about Cheryl's attitude. Cheryl's been over-stepping her role for one thing, and she hasn't been communicating properly regarding the interviews. She's also developed this hard, angry edge, some of it directed at Faith, and on one or two occasions, Faith's certain she caught a whiff of booze coming from Cheryl. Faith knows it can't have come to Anthea's attention yet, because Anthea would have dealt with it severely. What applies to the residents, applies to the staff. Even more so.

It all seemed to start when Cheryl had that funny turn, that time she had to lie down in the relaxation room, and Faith wonders if Cheryl's going through the change or something. She doesn't like to fight, preferring the consensus approach, but that's what she's had to do in order to carry out some of the follow-up interviews. Like the one she's hoping to do today, with Michael. "I'd like to interview him, Cheryl, if you don't mind," she said. "I was his key worker."

"Southampton, isn't it? That's not far for me to travel."

"It's not the distance. I just don't think he would let anyone else interview him."

She doesn't think she's ever known Cheryl look so inflamed, her dark eyes bright and formidable. She lit a cigarette, and it shook as she held it against her pencilled eyebrow. "Do you believe everything they tell you, Faith?"

Faith hesitated before replying. "Not everything, Cheryl. Of course not."

"Then how do you know what's lies and what's the truth?"

"Experience, I suppose. You get a sense for these things."

"But how can you rely on any of it?" Cheryl's cigarette was still quivering against her temples. "They're all so used to lying and manipulating– "

"If it gains them to lie, yes."

"Well then."

"But it doesn't mean everything they say is lies. Childhood experiences, for instance."

"Don't you think their memories are all wildly distorted? Their brains all addled with drugs? I bet if you interviewed their parents you'd get a totally different picture." The muscles in her neck were all flushed and taut, on the verge of spasm, and she was starting to scare Faith.

"I wouldn't want to interview some of their parents."

"See? You do believe everything they say. But there are two sides– " And then, her eyes filling up, she said, "Perhaps it's best you interview Michael, after all. I might just feel like throttling him."

"Cheryl…is everything all right?"

"Yeah yeah. I'll be fine."

"I'm not trying to step on your toes. You know, if you ever need to talk about anything, Cheryl, we all have personal stuff."

But Cheryl just stared at her, half-blank, half-nasty.

*

Faith parks her car. Michael has been difficult to trace, he's been pretty elusive since he left Chrysalis and though she enlisted the help of a local drugs agency worker to make contact with him on her behalf, she's not at all confident of getting any reply this afternoon as she knocks on the door.

Eventually a young girl comes to the door in her dressing gown, squinting at Faith with sleepy features, before getting her brain in gear. "Michael? Number 5, I think. Upstairs, first door on the left."

She climbs the stairs and at first it doesn't seem as if she's going to get an answer from Number 5, but then he appears at the door looking a bit scraggy and tremulous. He forgot she was coming today, that much is clear, but he lets her in anyway. He doesn't offer her a cup of tea, there isn't a kettle in the room as far as she can see, but even if there is, he doesn't look with it enough to think of such things. He sits cross-legged on the floor, sniffs a lot, and occasionally pats Woodstock's outstretched belly. But most of the time he stares dopily at the dusty tendril trailing from the incense holder on the carpet between them – one of those carpets that will never look clean again, no matter how much you scrub it. After a while he says, "What is it you've come for again?"

She explains again about the follow-up research.

"I'm no success story if that's what you're looking for." He smiles. "I just make a success of being a mess."

"We were all devastated to hear about Callum."

"You heard then? You just can't keep clean out here. We were doing great when we first left Chrysalis and then you just get, like, sucked back into it. I freaked when I found Callum ... it was too late."

"I'm sorry," she says, and Woodstock sits up and lets out a single bark, before settling back down on the gungy carpet.

At a suitable point, she starts to work through her checklist: current drug use, employment, housing, family support – and at the mention of his family he looks intently at the incense remains. "I just stand there and stare at the phone sometimes. That pay phone downstairs." Woodstock then makes a squeaky whine, crying don't they call it. "I even got as far as picking it up once, but I couldn't go through with it."

"Don't know where he is no more," he goes on. "He's moved. He could be anywhere."

"Who, your father?"

He doesn't answer, but she can see in his face that he's obsessed with his family in the same way that those without friends are sometimes desperate to make them.

"Don't know if he's alive even. Callum tried to think of ways I could trace him."

"You did try to contact him then?"

"Couldn't remember the phone number. We looked in the phone book but it was out of date and none of the addresses or numbers was right."

"Did you try his place of work?"

"Callum did for me – but nothing."

"What about your mother's place of work?" But he shakes his head quickly and dismissively. "She wouldn't want to know."

"I should try and find a current phone book."

"Yeah."

She wishes she could scoop him up close to her. She wants to draw him in tight and absorb some of it for him, because you can go on dissecting and dissecting but never quite reach it. If she could only hold him tight and not let go until she's squeezed it right out of him, whatever it is. But the Chrysalis tradition of hugging each other hello and goodbye has always left him feeling a bit uneasy and so she reaches into her folder instead.

"I picked this up at the library," she says.

"What is it?"

"A list of courses at the FE College. I thought you might be interested."

"Cheers," he says, Woodstock's muzzle at his lips.

"Go for it, Michael," she says. "You can do it."

BACKWARDS AND FORWARDS

1

Cards. Being a real student means lots of cards – NUS card, student railcard, library card. It means sharing a house with other students, though his room is still empty, apart from the bed and the standard lamp with its huge cooling-tower light shade, frilled with orange tassels. Whoever lived here before must have been pretty sound, anyway, because there's a half-ripped World Wildlife Fund sticker on one of the splintery drawers – the one that won't close properly even when you ram your whole weight against it.

He doesn't know the other students who live here, except to say hello to when they pass on the stairs or make cups of tea in the kitchen – and only one of them, Libby, is at the same college as him and she's doing A Levels. The rest are Higher Education students.

College isn't as bad as he thought. He just has to sit there and take notes on Music or Physics or History or English. What he doesn't like is hanging around in the refec during free periods. Lunchtime is worse, it draws in the crowds. He doesn't know anyone. It's his fault because he got the dates mixed up and started one week after everyone else and by the time he got here everyone else knew their timetables, which rooms were where, who their tutors were, which books to buy, and they all knew each other.

But it isn't like school. It's laid back. Lecturers with long hair who you call by their first names and it's really up to him whether he turns in or not and so he drops English. He already has an O Level in English anyway. He just thought he'd try the GCSE, try for a higher grade.

Music is his favourite. He lies across his bed doing his music homework, the radio making scratchy noises in the background. He should really learn the tin whistle, properly, to bring the theory to life. He used to mess around with one at Chrysalis now and again, in the woods and places.

It's not too hard the Music homework, just a few exercises working out some major keys. It's better than reading thick chapters or writing complicated essays, but there's a song playing on the radio. He's heard it before, just once or twice, and it's making him sit up and listen. Genesis. Singing, you're no son, you're no son of mine, when you walked out you left us behind. It's all there. All there in that one song, a personal message, and suddenly G major and its tones and semitones are totally irrelevant, they've been crowded out by this one fear. The fear that his father, if alive, won't want to know him. This is how it'll be. Because he ran away. He walked out. Like the song says.

For months he's been working towards this one end. He went to the library, shortly after Faith visited that time, and looked through the latest phone book – London residential (L-Z). He could rule them all out, except one. Only one fitted, matched his father's initials, the one in Tooting Bec, though a different road than the one he grew up in. But it took him weeks to pick up the phone and even then things kept working against him – bad weather or no 10ps or 20ps or 50ps or people-in-phone-boxes or queues-outside-phone-boxes or out-of-order phone boxes – and so he's only ever tried the number twice. Both times, no answer.

But he knows this is the number. This is the number and tonight is the night. The song is a sign and he goes off in search of a decent phone box, the quiet one, ten minutes away. But there's someone in it. There always is at half past seven. He hates waiting, hates it more than anything, but tonight he's glad to be let off the hook because he didn't want to make the call, not really, not tonight. He's about to turn round and go home when he sees the girl inside hang up. She's poking about under the metal flap for her unused coins, and now she's coming out. She's holding the door open for him.

He feels icy November blowing under the call box. There's a shiver in his head as he picks up the receiver and presses the metal buttons, clack clack clack.

They say that time is a healer
And now my wounds are not the same

A woman answers. Not his mother or sister and he hangs up fast. But who is she? A girlfriend? A friend? The cleaner?

*

It's not enough to hear. He needs to see with his own eyes. But now, as he leaves the tube at Tooting Bec, this Saturday, his legs start to feel unsteady. They get worse as he makes his way down residential, shipshape roads to what must be his father's house.

He's sheltered by the late afternoon dinginess of November as he approaches Number 53, with the black gates, but the lights are off. Come all this way and no one's home, but there's a wall at the bus stop opposite and a great sense of relief as he sits and calms down and waits for the mystery woman to appear.

But nothing, so he goes for a walk and the walking warms him up and gets him thinking about what he'll do if he sees the woman or his father at the house, but when he returns to Number 53, nearly half an hour later, it's still in darkness, though the houses on either side are fully lit. Maybe there's a match on at Selhurst Park today. Maybe that's where his father is, where both of them are. He waits for a while longer and then goes back to the tube.

*

The next casualty is History. What the hell was he thinking of when he signed up to do four subjects? He can't even hack three. Faith once said that taking drugs for years can screw up your powers of concentration, and now he's finding she was right, as she was about most things. Even two subjects is heavy going, though Physics and Music are more concrete, rather than verbal and subjective. In Music, there are definite right and wrong answers. Four semiquavers to a crotchet, two crotchets to a minim, a D flat is the same as a C sharp. Tone Tone Semitone, Tone Tone Tone Semitone. These are the rules for major keys. But even this is too technical. Too mechanical. He feels rhythm. Feels the beat. Thinking kills it. Tone Tone Telephone. The rhythm comes when it comes. Come on, Woodstock, let's go for a walk.

Libby is sitting on the bare wood stairs talking to a girlfriend with bright blond hair, as he passes with Woodstock. Libby likes Woodstock. She always makes a fuss of him, she likes to rub his ears and dog-sits at the drop of a hat. She's the only one in the house with some life about her. The others are too studious. Dead as cemeteries.

Tone Tone Telephone. The rhythm comes when it comes. The urge to ring that Tooting number is like the urge to stick needles in himself. The sort of urge that always ends in hurt, but sometimes he just can't help himself. Can't do a thing once he gets that woodpecker tap-tap.

Tonight the phone box is empty and as Woodstock settles on a floor of dried piss, Michael finds himself going on autopilot as he presses the numbers, tap tap. Engaged. And again. Again and again. Tone Tone Tone Tone. Again Again Again Again. Tone Tone Go Home. Six, ten, twelve times, he's losing count of the redials but this time it's going to ring because there's a different pause after he presses the numbers. Here they come. Shit-scary double rings. Tone Tone. Tone Tone. He wishes it would stop. Tone Tone. Could be that his hand slipped. Could be that it's a wrong number and if he dials again he'll bring back that safe busy tone and he wants to run but there's a huge click on the other end and he's about to make that connection–

Hullo? The voice on the other end is coming from yesterday and he cuts his father off quick.

*

When he gets back to the house, Libby and her blond friend are still sitting on the stairs, each of them taking it in turns to swig from a bottle of Newcastle Brown. "This is Catrina," says Libby. "She's moving in here after Christmas, when Clare moves out."

When Clare moves out. That's news to him. He didn't even know Clare was moving out. He doesn't even know Clare, as it goes. He doesn't really know anyone in the house, come to think of it. But Catrina looks the kind of girl who'll tip the balance. Who'll change things. Sort of arty, like she might shake up the house...

But he's got other things on his mind. Gnawing away at him, like a new addiction. He goes up to Tooting again the next Saturday, only this time it's daylight, only this time he's taken a spot of whizz which blasts through him like a firework. He feels like someone impatient for a bus, someone about to go dangerous and out of control because he's full of blood. Everything vibrates while he sits on the seat opposite, clutching his head, and there's a Red Sierra parked in the road outside the house, and after about twenty minutes, which might be forty minutes, someone appears from the side of the house and starts to walk briskly towards the black gates. Him. It's got to be, but he can't take a second look, though he hears the sing of the hinges as the gates open, and now no barrier separates them. No physical one. Get a grip, you stupid fucker. Get a grip. *I came here for help, I came here for you.* But the world's slipping out of focus and the static zzz zzz is in his ears and he just makes out the fuzzy figure closing the gates and heading for the Sierra. It's him all right, unlocking the car and climbing in. The hairline, the curve of his broad shoulders, who else's?

Get a hold of yourself. And his father starts up the car and drives right past him out of sight.

*

Can't concentrate on his Music. Simple time. Compound time. All the time. *Till it started happening all the time.* Intervals. Lost Time. Music is broken down into phrases. Like sentences or poems. That speak to him and him only. Phrases that won't leave him alone, but become fodder for the woodpecker in his head.

On the ninth of December, he and Woodstock are back on the train to Tooting. He hasn't dropped History, after all. History dominates his every thought. But December is dark and safe, good for hiding behind, and before he knows it he's on that seat again opposite Number 53. The lights are full on inside. He wonders whether the mystery woman is in there, pegging up Christmas cards on string or crêpe paper, like his mother used to, or doing the gravy just how his father likes it, rich and smooth, and he only came here to watch. But something's overtaking him and making him cross the road, it could be the darkness, or Woodstock, making him feel safe enough to stand at the gates.

Through the front window he sees a big Christmas tree in the lit lounge. Christmas is for other people, with proper families. For the rest, it's about getting wrecked, it's a bed on a church hall floor when the temperature hits freezing outside.

He goes through the gates and moves across the garden, for a different view. Everything looks so normal in there: the ornaments on the windowsill and above the gas fire. He sees some silver and crystal-glass glinting at him. Not that his father's ever been rich. Just comfortable. Oh and those guns he used to collect – they're on display in this house too, hanging above the fireplace. He'd forgotten all about those. Funny how the mind blots out the gross bits. If this was a film, he'd be expected to break in, take up one of the guns which would be loaded, of course, and blast his father to kingdom come. But he doesn't feel like that, and now he's standing bang outside the front door. It looks strange and scary up close, the shapes on the other side of the patterned glass like something in a kaleidoscope, and in a moment of madness he rings the bell. *I rang that bell with my heart in my mouth, I had to hear what he'd say.* And now the smaller parts are merging together, the panes filling up with one big greeny shape.

Him.

Opening the door.

Standing a few feet away.

For a split second, he's still incognito with his long hair and ragged look and then the penny drops, right there in his father's eyes.

And the sound of the penny dropping is as a gunshot to a rabbit.

2

Waterloo station was Michael's idea, on the phone, though they said little else. But here he can escape any time. Into the Christmas crowds. Through an exit. To the loos. Escape is very much in his head at the moment, because he can see his father, though his father hasn't spotted him yet. He's still sizing him up from this safe, half-hidden spot, looking at the thickened face and yellowing hair. He's still got the time to flee, but not the ability. His father's seen him now, anyway.

They don't know what to say, now they're face to face. His dad pats him on the shoulder, and after a while says, "I suggest we go and find somewhere a bit quieter. It's mayhem with all these Christmas shoppers."

"I wanna stay here."

"We could go to the station buffet."

"Yeah, that'll do."

"You get a seat then and I'll get us some drinks. Coffee OK?"

"Yeah. "

When his father comes back with the tray, he looks under the table at Woodstock. "I'm not sure if dogs are allowed in here."

"Tough."

"Had him long?"

"Few years. We go everywhere together."

There's an awkward silence.

"Can I get you a burger or something?"

"Don't eat meat."

"A veggie burger then? You look as if you could do with building up."

"Don't want nothing."

Another awkward silence.

"Mikey, are you in some kind of trouble?"

"No."

"Have you been sleeping rough or something?"

"No. I'm living with students."

"Students? So you're at college then?"

"Don't sound so surprised."

"What are you studying?"

"This and that. What are you up to these days anyway?"

His father leans back, loosens his overcoat. "I'm indulging my passion for boats. At the boatyard. I've been working there for, oh, close on four years now, it must be. Well, Air Traffic Control was becoming more and more stressful."

Michael spills his coffee everywhere. His dad makes an attempt to mop it up with one of the serviettes and gets him another. The spilled coffee has broken the ice, a little. His father removes his overcoat and answers the questions put to him without fluster. That will have been Jane who answered the phone. No, he hasn't heard from Michael's mother lately. She was working with some alcoholics in– ? Elaine would know. Elaine was living up at her place for a while. He expects Michael wants to see his mother, doesn't he, after all this time. No? Very well, if she should contact him for any reason he won't mention to her about today, or any of it, if Michael really doesn't want him to…

He hears news of Elaine and her boyfriend, of Stephen who's in Manchester, an Economics graduate and doing very well for himself in computers, bit of a high-flyer, doesn't keep in touch all that often. But he's not like Stephen, he's a low-flyer, in fact he's barely got off the ground, though college is a start, and now his dad's mentioning his half-sister, Juliet…

It's too much, his thoughts are wheeling like gulls. Beyond the café, he hears the lure of train doors slamming and looks up at the giant clock. He gets up. "I have to get back to Southampton," he lies. "I wanna get the five o'clock train."

They leave the buffet and wait for the south coast train. There's a feeling of unfinished business, or to be more precise, business not yet started. His dad is writing out Elaine's address and telephone number on the back of a manila envelope and he's also trying to persuade Michael to part with his Southampton address, but he isn't giving it. He wants to be the one in control. His father is saying he doesn't want for them to lose touch for another eight years. It was eight years of, he starts to say, still with that nervous blink as he speaks, and I did search for you, you know, after you suddenly left home…and anyway, why don't you come over for Christmas? It'll be just myself and Jane this year, but she'd like to meet you, I'm sure. We could get something vegetarian in for you if you don't eat turkey. Jane? Yes, she is my partner, that's right. Oh and do bring your girlfriend along too, if you have one.

So he's got his dad's permission to have a girlfriend now and he'll let him bring her home too.

Pity he ain't fucking got one as it goes.

"Think about it anyway," says his father as he reaches into his wallet and takes out fifty pounds. "Here," he says, still with the old bribes. "This should cover your train fare and a few hot meals."

Michael hesitates for a moment, he doesn't want his father's dirty money, but he takes it all the same.

*

It isn't Jane's fault, any of this. In fact Michael's sort of looking forward to meeting her. He doesn't intend spending Christmas with them: all that food and false festivity would be too much. Besides, he's more of a Solstice person himself so he's fitting them in today instead, on his way over to Elaine's who's spending Christmas with a friend at Gipsy Hill.

Jane turns out to be very different from his mother, thankfully. She's chatty – not in a nosey way – but in a pleasant background way. It's sort of lulling the way she talks. A voice good for babies and children and sick people. She's in her late thirties probably; dark-haired and undressy with big fleshy legs. He's relieved that she's there at all, providing as she does a welcome buffer between the claustrophobia of father and son. But she's too respectful of blood relationships that go back years and years. "I expect the two of you have a lot of catching up to do," she says, "so I'll make myself scarce."

No don't do that for fuck's sake, Michael thinks, stay here. Stay right here. But she's already closing the door behind her and there's an awkward few moments when neither father nor son know what to say. Oh, his dad's just remembered, I've got something to tell you, Michael. It sounds so rehearsed, so falsely spontaneous but they're saved by the bell of the telephone ringing across the lounge. As his father speaks into it Michael tries not to scan the contents of the cabinets too closely but he can't help himself. He feels repulsed all of a sudden, by this nasty compulsion to convert valuables into ready cash but once a junkie always a junkie don't they say and it's his mother on the other end, he can tell by the way his father shifts uneasily from one foot to the other as he speaks to her. She still controls him then, even in their separation, even in spite of Jane.

Michael wonders what his mother would say if she knew he was here. Would she be surprised? Interested? Angry? Indifferent? Does she even mention him in her conversations with his dad? Or has she altogether wiped him from her life; written him off as a bad job? Funny how the mind blots out the gross bits, the bad things in life, the failures. If he could just stop shaking enough to walk over tot he phone and say something to her, anything, sorry would be s start, but he'd only come across as stupid, he'd only dither and quiver and blither and anything else that rhymes and anyway his dad's hanging up now and is swift to get in first. "As I was saying, I've got something to say to you. I want to get you a car, it'll be secondhand of course but I'll see to the tax and insurance." A car? Michael can't hide his interest. "And I've also got a proposal to make. I've spoken with someone at work about some Saturday employment for you, starting after Christmas if you want it, because I know how hard up you students can get. It might be a bit mundane to begin with, tidying up and lifting, maybe checking plant equipment and so forth, but it'll give you a few extra quid each week and who knows, it might lead to something more interesting. There are courses and apprenticeships..."

He adds: "Of course, you'd be welcome to stay here at weekends..."

Michael desperately needs the cash, his dad knows this, and sweeping up an old boatyard and hosing down a few boats, well, that doesn't sound too taxing and he'll have no living costs each weekend if he stays up here; that alone would make it worthwhile, and a car, his very own, well, that's the carrot, isn't it?

3

When Elaine opens the door of her friend's Gipsy Hill flat, she beams at Michael. Then they embrace. It's been too long.

"Dad did warn me…it's your hair, Michael…that's what it is."

"That's what what is?"

"Why you look so different. "

"So do you."

"Come in. My friend's out doing some Christmas shopping so she'll be a while yet." She grabs a bottle of wine and corkscrew from a kitchen worktop, nudges a door open.

"You go in there, I'll just get a couple of glasses." She hands him the bottle and corkscrew. "You can open the bottle. I'm hopeless with corks."

He laughs. "So am I."

When she returns with two misty glasses she places them on the floor between them. "Give it here."

She takes the bottle from him and they both laugh as the cork crumbles and shreds on its tortuous route from the bottle neck.

She pours them both a glass and sits against the wall with her knees up. He sits cross-legged on the floor opposite against the settee, which is full of Christmas decorations and other festive paraphernalia. Cigarettes are rolled and lit.

They chat and laugh and drink the wine and become more bold and drink the wine. He's never been a wine drinker.

Suddenly Elaine says: "You do drugs, don't you?" And his head feels too fuddled to deny it and then she says, "Confession time. So do I. Or I did do. But I'm clean at the moment. That's why I'm staying here." She gives him a reassuring look. "It's OK. I won't say anything to anyone. It's no surprise anyway – you using. You can't disappear for so many years without people thinking something."

It's now emerging that their dad searched squats and all sorts looking for Michael. Sometimes he and Elaine feared the worst – drink, drugs, prison, overdose – though it was never spoken about outright, not once the initial commotion of his leaving home had died down. Their mother said he'd stolen from them and she'd sent him packing.

"But I knew there had to be more to it than that."

She's now looking at Michael, square on. She's about to come out with something terrifying and personal, something that's been bugging her. Something he doesn't want to hear but the wine is gently dissolving both their senses.

"There's something else," she goes on. "Something I've known for years. Putting two and two together I worked out why you left home." He waits for the hammer to fall. "You knew dad had been seeing another woman, didn't you? It just became obvious that mum thought you'd somehow been in on the secret. You know, lying for him and stuff."

"Is that what she said?"

"It just seemed as if she was as angry with you as she was with him, then the way you suddenly left home like that and the way mum was suddenly calling dad all the filthy names under the sun. I guessed you'd had a big bust up over it. Mum refused to discuss it or you after she'd sent dad packing. It all started to slot into place when dad agreed to leave without a fuss so I guessed he had to be the guilty one."

She divides the remaining wine into their glasses, taking the lion's share for herself.

"Mum banned dad from the house and tried to stop him from seeing me and Stephen. It was way over the top. Mum was so angry and venomous but you know what she can be like."

Oh he knows, all right.

"It did all blow over after a while, but then dad started to go downhill. He began to drink and look unshaven – not much – just a bit unkempt sort of thing. Then he lost his job."

"Lost it? I thought he jacked it in."

"Well, he would say that, wouldn't he? That's what he wants everyone to believe, but I reckon he got the push. I felt sorry for him back then."

She glugs back the rest of her wine. "Now it's all different, of course. He's doing all right for himself, he's doing what he always wanted to do – you know, with the boats and stuff – and he's met Jane. She's lovely, Jane. And mum and dad are on quite good terms these days. You can only be angry for so long, I guess, that's what I think anyway. All that other stuff seems to be behind them, it's never mentioned anyway, and they seem to get on better now. Funny, isn't it? They've both got their own lives now. I was living in the same house as her with my ex until a few months ago."

She snatches a straggly piece of red tinsel from the floor, winds it round her wrist a few times, making a bracelet of it.

"I think mum may have been seeing that Peter de Cruz bloke for a while. I don't know. I don't see much of mum or dad, to be honest. I've got my own life, my own circle of friends. Being around mum gets sort of – poisonous. Know what I mean?"

He does that.

"What about Stephen? See anything of him? "

She shakes her head, a bit wistful. "Nah. Stephen went through a bad patch himself when mum and dad first split up. He lost weight and had this mystery virus for months but he threw himself into his studies and now it's his career. His life's in Manchester with his girlfriend. He hardly comes south any more. He deliberately makes himself busy at family times, like Christmas."

She gets up from her place on the floor. Clears one box of Christmas decorations from the sofa. "He once told me, God years ago now, how he hated coming home from school in the holidays because he hated the way mum made such a fuss of him. He hated the way it alienated him from us. Can you imagine?"

So it wasn't all in his head. And Elaine had nobody, but he doesn't feel sorry for her. He envies her. She was lucky. Very lucky, never having to shoulder the burden of favouritism.

4

A few days before Christmas, Michael goes to the boatyard with his father, to be shown around and to get a feel for the place. The other men at the boatyard find him a bit strange at first though they go out of their way to help him seeing as he is who he is: the son of Andrew. Funny how Andrew's always been quiet about his family life but his son clearly needs a helping hand, a start on life, and they're happy to oblige.

Michael does whatever small job he's asked to do and when he needs reviving he secretly gives himself a little jab of something. Just a very little so that he'll appear keen and confident and unlazy, and at the end of that first day the ruddy-faced bearded yard manager called Sid tells him that he's worked hard today, laddie, and that it just goes to show that you shouldn't judge a leopard by his spots – not all lads with long hair are layabouts, and maybe they should find out more about these government scheme Employment Training whatsits, whatever they call them these days.

After work, Michael goes with his father to check out a used car advertised in the paper. A fifteen-year-old Vauxhall Viva, as it goes. His father asks the relevant questions and they take it for a test-drive.

"What d'you reckon then, Mikey? Apart from a few touches up to the bodywork here and there, all seems to be in good working order for a car this age."

"I ain't earned any reddies yet."

"I know... but I promised you a car. Call it an early Christmas present. Are you spending Christmas with me and Jane?"

"Nah...I have to get back. But I'll be up here again to start at the yard in the new year."

By the time Michael gets back to his father's, he's ready to crash on the settee, he's starting to come down...

When he wakes, ages later, it's daylight outside and he heads off back to Southampton for Christmas.

*

The new housemate, Catrina, brought some of her stuff over to the house on Christmas Eve, though she didn't move in proper until after Christmas. As soon as she did, things started to feel different.

Her room's at the top of the stairs, Michael passes it on the way to his, but when Clare lived here the door was always closed for quiet study and you never knew if she was in or out. Now the door is open – it's already Catrina's door with its painted flowers and bright stickers – and when you pass you can see right in to her colourful den of scarves and mobiles and incense. The other day he caught her ironing her flowing skirt without even taking it off. She just lifted it up and looped it over the ironing board.

"Hi Michael," she said, unfazed. "Come in and have a proper look at my room. It feels like home now," she said, and he stepped inside among all the treasures, unable to take it all in. There was so much to experience. Beautiful beady bags, hanging from every door handle, and Joni Mitchell playing on the turntable. "You've got good taste in music," he told her. She sat on the bed surrounded by literature classics – the Brontës, Jane Austen, Thomas Hardy – and he wished he'd stuck at English, so that he'd have something intelligent to say on the matter. She was making herself a patchwork waistcoat. There were lots of pins all standing in a circle on the carpet and he said, "Oh look, pinhenge!" and she laughed. Well, that was something. Making her laugh.

These are his two lives: the one in Southampton and the weekends in London at the boatyard with his father. When in London he keeps the images of Catrina's bewitching ways in a box in his head, ready to summon if needs be.

There's definitely something to be said for surrounding yourself with boats, anyway. Just the sight of them makes you want to sail off somewhere; promises adventure, but tonight he's feeling uneasy back here at his father's house, just the two of them, no Jane. He's still not clear what the set-up is as far as Jane goes, whether she's intending to sell her own house and move in with his dad or not. He's gathered there are still practical and financial things to sort out from her first marriage.

He feels safest sprawled out in the enclosure of an armchair where he's been sitting since seven o'clock, watching TV, rolling his cigarettes. He can't move. If he stays welded to his chair he might just suspend the world around him, or freeze it, or annihilate it. All the same he still feels on tenterhooks the whole time as if in dread of spiders or creepy things. Maybe the world has frozen him. Certainly whenever his father brings him food or cups of coffee Michael keeps his eyes firmly fixed on the screen. He hopes his body language is correct and Chrysalis-approved and conveying what it's supposed to convey and suddenly he remembers that dream message from some years ago: strength is distance. Yes. If he can just be strong mentally like the little girl...he now wishes he'd have brought Woodstock instead of leaving him behind with Libby and Catrina. Woodstock is both barrier and protector, but he couldn't really take Woodstock along to the boatyard so figured he was best left with the girls, and now, at last, his father announces that he's ready for bed; there's a bed upstairs for Michael, if he wants it. He'll probably crash down here, he says, so his father brings him some blankets and says goodnight.

He knows it's going to be a long night but he can at least make himself more at home, now that his father's out of the way. He can stretch his legs for one thing and make himself a hot drink and spread out on the settee with the blankets.

He dozes, he wakes to the sounds of some tacky chat show, dozes, wakes again – enough to switch off the telly, dozes. He wakes shivering, the blankets mostly on the floor. His chest feels tight, a bit asthmatic. He sips at his now cold coffee on the floor.

He feels, or imagines he feels, the enchanting long blond hair of Catrina sweeping his face; and her deep blue eyes – or are they green? – smiling at him to take that leap forward with her. In his dreams!

But now every creak in the house is reminding him of older spirits, ones that creep and whisper *Just a little more for Mr Ray, then you can get up and play* – but as soon as he becomes fully awake the lounge is always empty, the door always closed as before.

At the hush of dawn, and now fully awake, he no longer feels jittery or delirious but an emotional compound of confusion, loss and loneliness, or something even more indefinable. Outside, Sunday is stirring, what is he waiting for? The car, the Viva, his very own, its roof covered in a film of winter like all the others at the roadside, is there for the driving. Sunday is stirring and he quietly slips away.

*

Tuesday evening and he must be in a dream, because he's sitting very close to Catrina in her lamplit bazaar. They're on the bed because there's nowhere else to sit, her only chair heaving with the scarves and skirts and things. It all started the night before, when she found him slumped in the bathroom with his hand cut, after that student bash that he got dragged along to. There were other students there cracking jokes he didn't understand, picking apart books he's never read or never likely to read, and raving about films he's never heard of. He went to the toilets, he remembers that much, to shoot up a bit of confidence so he could join in and say something cool to Catrina.

The rest is a bit of a blur, until the bathroom. She was dressing his wound and asking why, and he lied. "It's the booze," he said. "It, like, makes me black out and do mad things if I have too much." Past experience has told him that folk are better about booze than they are with drugs.

And now they're closer. Really close. She's sitting here telling him he's really sweet. "I like guys who are sort of lost," she says. "In fact," she says, twiddling one of the two and a half buttons left on his shirt, "I find your insecurity a turn-on. D'you know that?"

He doesn't. No one's ever said anything like that and she starts to undo the buttons but he's scared about the things she might find – the pock marks and old sores and track marks – so he ducks under the bedclothes next to her, and after they've made love she sits up naked in bed. Naked except for her floppy green velvet hat which they've been taking it in turns to wear all evening. They listen to The Doors and Jimi Hendrix and music from the generation they wish they'd grown up in, and Angus across the hall knocks sheepishly on the door at 1am and asks if they'd mind turning the music down a bit because he's got a nine o'clock start in the morning.

They, on the other hand, don't give a toss about missing their lectures and she wants him there at night to make love with, wants their red hot thighs to burn against each other, wants him there to talk and laugh and listen to music with right into the small hours and he wants these things too. He's never felt so high. He wants it to stay like this always.

He starts to increase his speed intake. Furtively. To satisfy that passion of hers.

Then, by chance, one evening, she says to him, "Have you ever wondered what heroin's like? It's supposed to make you sexy, isn't it?"

"It'll probably make you puke if you've never had it before. Speed's the stuff."

"Really? Can you get us some?"

But he makes a big mistake getting her into speed, because it only increases her sexual appetite and as the weeks go by, he needs more and more of the stuff to keep up with her. Her dainty bite-sized snorts have a huge effect on her, but she makes it look pretty and harmless, like a glass of champagne. She's just a social user, not an addict, but if she ever finds out the truth about him she'll come down on him, for sure, and he smiles to himself because this is what she likes to do in bed, come down on him, though sometimes she wants him to be a man and then he feels as if he's competing with her ex, Mr Zen, who was something of a stud, by all accounts.

And drugs are also threatening to sabotage his weekend job which perhaps isn't such a bad thing in the circumstances because he's being plagued by all manner of odd feelings towards his father: awkwardness and frustration at what's left unsaid; anger at the thought of being too old at twenty-four to do 'those things' any more; guilt at sometimes longing for that closeness and physical affection again. But what he wants most of all is some sort of acknowledgment, an apology, some sort of justice. He wants these things badly but he's only getting material reparation. Perhaps this is his father's way of saying sorry or perhaps it's all a bribe, in the old way, to buy his silence.

The Vauxhall Viva is already a write-off from driving it when he was out of his tree one time and then one weekend when he does manage to make it in to the boatyard, one of the men finds him crashed out in one of the boats – (the one called Allegra and said to be jinxed because if anything goes wrong it's nearly always Allegra though Michael feels he could quite happily live on her) – and reports it to Sid. That evening his father says: "Sid thinks you're on drugs, Michael." And Michael finds himself saying: "Drugs? Where the fuck did Sid get that idea from? I'm just shattered from this job and all the travel and the study." But his father's not buying it. "It all makes sense now," he says. "The smashed up car, the unreliability, those marks on your arms…I saw them once when you were asleep on the couch." Michael grows hot and defensive. "They ain't nothing, those marks. So I did drugs once or twice, years ago, but I was never hooked." He's become a good liar over the years. He hopes he's convinced his father it was a thing in the past, a phase that he's grown out of.

But there are more incidents. He's beginning to blow his cover, he's becoming forgetful and morally suspect.

"I can't understand where that rose-bowl's gone," his dad says to Jane one Saturday night. "And something else used to be there on the mantelpiece." And Jane says: "Wasn't it the carriage clock? Oh it'll be Daisy from Number 47. She's getting more and more confused. She puts things in her bag and then forgets she's done it. She was here the other day. It's a bit delicate, isn't it? Shall I phone her daughter? " And Michael, scarlet with guilt and rage, pulls the phone right out of the wall because they're playing games with him, to trap him, to get him to own up, and as he slams the door behind him he thinks of Catrina and starts to calm down. He wishes the Easter holidays would hurry up and finish. He's counting off the days when she returns from her mother's…

*

But when Catrina returns a fortnight later it's with a different attitude. "I've got to knuckle down to it, Michael," she says. "You can't piss about with A Levels."

If she catches him hovering in the doorway, she'll say it again. "I've got so much to do, Michael. Haven't you?"

He hasn't. He can't tell her that he's now dropped Physics and is pinning all his hopes on Music. She wouldn't understand. She's an A Level student, like Libby, one of those clever people practising for the real McCoy: university or art college. So he sits in his room, twiddling with the orange tassels on the great cooling-tower lamp while pretending to study.

Soon after, he loses his Saturday job in London. He had it coming. They don't want to dismiss him, Sid tells him after one of the men called Tommy found him with a loaded syringe ready for the shoot, but they've got no choice. It's too dangerous in an environment like this. He could have a nasty accident. He could fall off the wharf into the canal – anything. Perhaps when he's sorted himself out a bit, they'll reconsider his position.

Back at his dad's, he's having to explain himself again.

"Michael, why didn't you tell me you were an addict?"

"I didn't want to let you down."

"You've not let me down."

"Yeah I have. You won't be able to show your face at work now that they know you've got a junkie for a son."

"I'm not worried about that. You need help. Sid and the men understand that. There are places people like you can get themselves straightened out, aren't there?"

"Tried them all."

"Well, we can start by chucking the nasty stuff down the toilet. What is it anyway? Heroin?"

"Speed."

"I thought everyone took heroin or crack these days. What does speed do for you then?"

"Makes me feel good."

"You don't look very good, Mikey, if you don't mind me saying so."

"I do mind, as it goes."

"And what about AIDS? Aren't you worried about that?"

What the fuck does AIDS matter, or any of it, come to that?

So much has been happening these past few months: first college, then his father, and now Catrina. She's taken his mind off his father and all that old stuff, but sometimes it creeps in again, at nights. He'll lie awake for hours, imagining himself with a net. Casting it deep into the waters where emotions swim about like fish. He'll catch sight of one, awkwardly beating about the coral. Then another, a fat red fish, lashing its tail this way and that, and look another, a slow, deep-sea swimmer, gnawing away at the undergrowth. But most of all he imagines himself trawling the waters for a why. Did his father pass this way too? Did it happen to him? There was that funny uncle, there was the children's home, maybe it started there. All he wants is something to hang on to, like a route, a map describing his journey here, otherwise he's lost, nothing, annihilated. But all he's heard is the same old junk, the small talk, the money, the car. It's too late to challenge the past. The dark loft is still taboo and perhaps it always will be because he's now just another deranged drug addict. They all rant and rave, don't they? Tell big lies. They don't know what they're saying, druggies, they say horrible, outrageous stuff. They don't mean to but it's those evil drugs talking. Oh yeah, all so very neat. They've got him boxed and labelled and forever damned but his father wants to help him, he's offering him a refuge here, away from the Southampton drug scene, and Michael wants to stay. He needs time out. He doesn't want to face the music and sit the exam, no way. This is the perfect cop-out and his dad's promised him a camper van for his birthday if he promises to give up drugs and though he hates birthdays he would love a camper van. It would be like owning a pair of wings. It would impress Catrina, no end.

*

At the end of May, Michael returns to Southampton, clean, and looking forward to summer. He tells Catrina he's got a surprise for her.

She looks up from her revision. Even her writing paper is brightly coloured. It's a memory aid, she says. In her mind's eye, she tells him, she can picture the pink pages and the blue pages and the yellow pages with their various headings. She's clever like that, dead organized.

"It's outside," he tells her.

When she sees the camper van she falls in love with it as he hoped.

"Oh, wow, Michael, we can go travelling in the summer! Just think, we could take off to Glastonbury and hippy hang-outs in Wales before I go to art college."

*

Once on the road in the new van, painted up with bright naive flowers, Catrina's herself again. Exams behind her, they can drive

133

around, just the two of them, no other distractions.

She gives him back that nature wonder. "Look what the rain's brought out," she'll say, picking up a worm and wiggling it in his face.

"An earth dance does the same job," he'll say. "Me and Nicky used to make them come up when we went camping."

"You and Nicky," she'll repeat, though he's not sure what she means by it, if anything.

She spends large chunks of time just lying out, cloud-watching. "See those grey clouds?" she says. "They're the rocks and the patches of blue sky are the rock pools." Or she'll read out poems she's written about cirrus clouds like ridgy sand when the tide's gone out. Clouds are the earth's insulator, she writes and she's dead right – if clouds come down in the afternoon, they don't shiver at night.

As the days and nights pass, she grows more and more irritated by time that's watched or counted or measured, man-made time as she calls it, and in a fit of protest, chucks her watch down a grid. She wants to tell the time by lengthening shadows and feelings in her bones, she says. Like the ancients. Ways that have stood the test of time. Stone circles and signs in the hedgerows and rings on tree stumps, and he gets a flashback of his quartzy, clock-heart, twinkling like crystal.

"Feel the power of the elements," she says one evening, staring into their campfire. "What do you see in the flames, Michael?"

He sees Strength. Danger. Colour.

Water is her favourite. Fresh water is like silence, she says. Pure, clean, unadulterated.

The cold of the stream drains his craggy feet white and they laugh as they pull each other down and soak each other with showers.

Woodstock's all right, isn't he?

Yeah he loves the water.

The days become warmer still and they pitch the tent which gets oven-hot in the daylight hours, so they flake out in the sun or the shade and argue about whose turn it is to fetch water or wood or to cook, though they're too hot for real arguments. The heat is frying their brains and they only start to revive once the shadows slant and lengthen. Then they sit up and drink more water and go for a walk until the dark clouds of evening when they think about food, and the firelight and torchlight and beer and an extra pullover, maybe.

Catrina says this is what's meant by living creatively. Pitch here today, move on tomorrow. Anything that's yesterday's we'll leave behind. There's no place for souvenirs and sentimentalism in Catrina's world. It's all clutter, she says. It all belongs to the Great

134

Indoors and people suffocating under the weight of one place and too many yesterdays. Instead of many places and only one time. And that time is now. Travel is great for living in the now, she says. Visit here, live it to the full. Visit there.

If you can carry it, keep it, she says to him. She allows herself just a few small luxuries, like her crystals, which she cleanses on the waning moon (or is it the waxing?) and her oil-burner for burning her ylang ylang oil, but she tries to use up things if she can, otherwise the van will get too cluttered. "If we burn down the candles, we'll be lighter, Michael."

By night inside the tent, there's the beam from the torch and the sound of zips and the smell of cooped-in grass, and water hasn't had a chance to leak in yet, though plenty arcs outwards when he pisses out the evening's beer or lager. "It's all right for you, Michael," she'll moan. "You don't have to squat down on dewy thistles." Then she'll look up and say, "Hey, just look at the stars! The Plough and Orion's Belt ... so bright and clear without the streetlights. We must buy a book on the stars when we pass through the next town. Just a kid's book will do."

Woodstock's all right, isn't he?

He will be. Once he's inside my sleeping bag.

*

One day, she decides she wants to go to Sidmouth folk festival, but when they arrive she gets the hump with him, so he loses himself in the summery sights and sounds. Accordions and fiddles and juggling and hair-braiding.

She's so tired and sticky and thirsty, she's not stopped complaining about it, but five minutes into her lager and she's still not refreshed. "I still can't understand why you didn't take your exams," she says. "That was a total waste. Look at all these people who've got it together. Doesn't it make you want to do something with your life?" He looks away, hoping her mood will lift. "Sometimes I think that if there was only one unemployed person left in the world, you'd be it," she says, and she isn't smiling. Other travellers and festival-goers come under attack too. Even their animals. Especially their animals. "I mean, why do they always have to have dogs? And why are they always whippet-type dogs? Why not poodles or dachshunds?" He frowns. He doesn't have a clue what it's all about, this funny mood of hers. "It's because they think poodles are so unhip, isn't it?" she says. "The dogs are a uniform. It's pathetic. And why are they always black dogs?"

"Woodstock's black," he says.

"Well, why didn't you get a brighter one?"

"Because they don't come rainbow-coloured," he says, but this doesn't make her smile either. He doesn't know what's got into her, but he knows he doesn't want to upset her over something he said or did or didn't do. She's brought meaning to his life. Deep and special. If she ever left him, he'd be gutted, so he makes an extra effort not to cross her and it works for a while.

Until she stumbles across a syringe, one day, in a squashed coke can. She shakes it out and screeches at him, a bit like his mother used to.

"It's not mine," he says, but she isn't having any of it – she's way too smart.

"Where's your head at? Dope, a bit of snorting – all right – but needles? Needles are different. You're risking my life as well as yours. Don't you care about that?"

"I only done it the once. And I've never shared works."

"Works? Works?" Her nose is screwed up in outrage. "How do you know all these expressions, anyway?"

When he does eventually calm her down, she says she'll overlook it, this once, but if she ever, repeat ever, finds another she will–

He knows what she'll do. She'll leave him.

*

Now, every time they make trips back to Southampton or to her mother's in Newbury, she brings something back with her. Some small souvenir. Or photograph. Sentimentality is allowed then, as long as it's portable. Oh look at me in this one, eating that daffodil, she will say. I was so wild then, when I was with Mr Zen. This is my favourite of all time. This one of me lying naked in the snow. The high heels were Mr Zen's idea. We used to bounce ideas off each other – me and Mr Zen. He was pure inspiration, that man.

There's nothing else to do, anyway, on a pissing-it-down day, except look at photos. And within the confines of a small area, no larger than a veal crate, they argue.

"It's about time I saw you without a stitch on," she says, pulling at his waistband.

"Get lost."

"I've never seen you properly in the buff. Come on. Don't be shy."

"I don't want to, all right?"

"No need to get shirty. I've never known a man so shy about his body. Now Mr Zen, he couldn't keep his clothes on!"

"Mr Zen this, Mr Zen that. All I ever hear about is Mr fuckin'

Zen."

"Well, why can't you be more demonstrative? Why do I have to make all the moves?"

"You're always pushing me away, that's why."

"No, I'm not."

"Yes, you are."

"Only when I think you've been taking drugs."

"You take them too."

"Yeah but I do mainly organic stuff," she says. "A bit of grass here, a few mushrooms there. Anyway, I'm not talking about the stuff we do together. I mean, you sneaking off and taking them behind my back. I don't want you coming on to me, just because you're out of your tree."

"You don't like me without them. You say I'm too passive, so I can't win, can I?"

"You see? Now's a perfect example. This could have been fun – the rain streaming down outside, us all cosy in here."

"It's cold."

"See? You kill it dead every time." She gives him a knowing look. "Maybe it's not your fault."

"Meaning?"

"Nothing."

"No, go on."

"Well, maybe it's your background. Your parents."

"What the fuck have they got to do with it?"

She's staring at him now. Like she can see through his skin to the muck below. "You're always so evasive about them," she says. "And you never contact them."

"I was just living for the now, like you said. Just enjoying the time with you, not worrying about nothing or no-one else."

"That's a teensy bit selfish, don't you think? I mean, I think of my mum every day and you've seen how often I phone or write to her, and you see her whenever we go to Newbury."

"So?"

"So why can't I ever meet your parents? Are you ashamed of me or something?"

"Course not."

"Are you ashamed of them then? Is that it?"

"I don't have much to do with them, as it goes."

"Why? Have they done something awful to you? I've often wondered."

And so it goes on until her A Level results, but they are a relief, of sorts. Anything to stop the relentless tide of questions.

"I've passed them all, Michael. Two B's and a C." She jumps with delight. "Yippee, Michael! I'm going to Art College."

5

In their new Southampton flat, Catrina buzzes with her new course.
– We're doing ceramics this week.
– Futurism this week.
– Silk-screen painting this week.
– I'll be late home. We've got life drawing tonight.
"It's a foundation course," she explains. "We have to cover every aspect this term, so we'll know where to specialize next term." Then she looks at him for longer than a few seconds, something she hasn't done since the start of her course. "Why don't you resit your GCSE's, Michael? Then we'd both be doing something."

He promises to think about it, but the impetus gets buried somewhere under her half-squeezed acrylics and oils with congealed lids, her primed canvasses. He can't really do anything, except look on in wonder at her produce, brilliant and bold, growing from tiny seeds in her head. She's more than an ideas person, her ideas materialize, and the more meaning and purpose there is to her life, the less there seems to be to his. Their lives are diverging. He's beginning to get under her feet. She needs room to spread out and express herself, she says, and starts to get picky with him again. "You quiver and sleep all day, just like Woodstock," she says. "They say owners become like their pets after a while."

But it isn't really the sleeping all day that gets to her – when he's in bed she has the space to herself, at least, and the peace. "What I really can't hack is you moping about the flat all day doing nothing," she says. "I'm going to have to chuck you out while I work. I just can't concentrate otherwise."

And she's true to her word. She turfs him outdoors so he starts to trudge the streets and bumps into old junkies and gets up to no good, while she fills the air at home with powerful fumes and leaves pink thumbprints all over the paintwork. But he has a sort of resigned respect for what she's doing and learns to leave her alone in the flat for long periods at a time.

Then her period of self-confinement lessens. She starts working on a photography project with some other students which takes them out and about, wind and shine, evenings and weekends, and so he returns indoors and listens to Nirvana all day, loud and tortured, a soul screaming in pain, *Here we are now, entertain us.* He doesn't really have any friends outdoors, anyway. Not friends in the way Catrina has friends. Catrina has Blue and Miranda and they paint full frontals of male models on Thursday evenings. And she has Russell. Russell who's also part of this photography thing. Whose name keeps cropping up all over the place. Russell says this, Russell says that, for God's sake Russell's just a friend. That's what happens when you go to college, Michael. You meet new people and make new friends and you do projects together. It's fun.

Oh it's fun all right. She's having a ball. Anyone can see that. She's looking all rosy and fired up, like she was when he first met her. The truth's hitting home. Hitting him square in the chest, like a pain. She's the lovely Catrina surrounded by friends with exotic names and Bohemian art tutors and well-hung models, bearing their all on Thursdays. She's out where she should be – filming autumn scenes in the New Forest with Russell and Blue and the others. She's a go-getter, he thinks as he stuffs some things into a carrier bag and starts up the van. A go-getter, making the most of herself and her talents. Squeezing the tubes while he goes down them.

*

He heads off to Glastonbury. He climbs the Tor and hears didgeridoos and fills up plastic bottles with water from the White Spring and the Red Spring and this is the only thing he's getting high on – the healing water.

"She'll be proud of me, eh Woodstock?"

They drift along, him and Woodstock, and he thinks of Catrina all the time. He thinks of all her little reflections on life and how she once said that ordinary things, like newsagents and launderettes and last night's sick on the pavement, look out of place in Glastonbury, and even the graffiti has New Age overtones; that it's hard to believe that some people actually live here all the year round; that some people have lived here all their lives.

He thinks of her in Wells and in Salisbury and at Stonehenge. Poor Stonehenge, shut inside ropes and clicked at by Japanese and American and German tourists with their state-of-the-art cameras, and he thinks of her pins arranged in a henge on the carpet and her Aladdin's cave bedroom. He thinks of his first girlfriend Louise and their walks together in the park or watching the Saturday morning pictures. He thinks of Nicky and Judd with his walking stick and checked cap and Freddie clicking his fingers in the empty ironmonger bath. He thinks of Neil and Mr G and Callum, and Faith who always showed him real concern, and how at Chrysalis they strip you bear, sand you down and then help renovate you, first with a fresh undercoat and then a good-as-new finish, and he thinks of his mother and wonders whether she's still got that fierce, north-facing look. He'd like to be a fly on the wall – to see her without being seen. Maybe one day, when he's got it together a bit more, maybe then he'll surprise her, maybe then he'll just turn up on her doorstep, wherever that is, and they'll talk man to woman, and it's important to carry positive memories, as Faith taught him, positive memories of her singing the blues, and she used to look so happy and intense when she sung, dead dramatic. It was like the evening sun lighting up a north wall, and when she was happy, everyone was happy, everything was all right with the world, but it's been over a week since he's seen Catrina, and the Chalice Well water won't be fresh any more.

But the break's cleared his head and Catrina will have had time to miss him.

*

"Sorry for just fucking off like that," he says on his return. "I needed some time on my own."

"Yeah well," she says. "I've been doing some serious thinking myself."

"Here you are." He offers her his biggest plastic bottle. "Some water from the Chalice Well."

She looks at the bottle with disdain. "It's all cloudy."

"Yeah, sorry about that…anyway, we've both missed you, haven't we, Woodstock?"

"Look, I won't beat about the bush," she says, putting the water down on the table. "But I've decided to live in a student house again."

"Oh right. Whatever."

"You know, where I have my own room and everything." She folds her arms. "In fact, I've already found somewhere."

"You don't waste no time, do you? So what about me?"

"I'm sure you can find someone else to move in here."

"I mean, what about us? I thought we were a couple."

"Look, Michael, I'm under a lot of pressure at college. I just can't put the time into our relationship as I could."

"I need you, Catrina. You're good for me. I thought about you all the time I was away."

She turns away from him. "My course is so intensive. You know it is."

"So, I've given you the space, haven't I?"

"It's just not a good idea – you and me under the same roof."

"Says who?"

"Says me. I've achieved a lot more on my own. Anyway, you were the one who just took off without so much as a note or a phone call."

"I said I was sorry, didn't I?"

"What was I supposed to do? Just put my life on hold until you felt like showing up?" She picks up her spiral-bound notebook. Rips a sheet from it. "Look, I want us still to be friends. I'll give you my new address so you can come and see me – sometimes."

"Oh I get it. Excuse me if I'm a bit slow."

"You've lost me."

"Oh I know I've lost you, Catrina. To him, that's who. That Russell wanker. You're seeing him, ain't you? See? You can't even deny it, can you?"

"Oh grow up."

*

He parks his van across from the Art College in the four o'clock December murk. There she is, and that's bound to be Russell, that bloke she's walking very close to, that bloke who isn't her type at all, with his piddly beard and glasses and dark coat. Too serious. Too sensible. Too boring. They'll be holding hands any minute, just you wait, and now she's seen the van and so has Russell. Oh shit, she's probably saying, shit, it's Michael. And Russell is saying, you go over and humour him and I'll meet you at the usual in ten minutes, okay?

The bastard.

He starts up the van, but Catrina's legging it over here. She's panting slightly as she opens the door on the passenger side. She looks stunning in her black fitted coat and velvet hat as she climbs up and sits beside him.

"Turn the engine off," she says.

"Is that him?"

"Who?"

"Russell."

She doesn't answer. She doesn't have to. Her face says it all.

"You can do better."

"What are you doing here, Michael?"

"I want to see you again."

"You are seeing me."

"I mean go out with you."

She takes a long look at him. "You'd only drag me down. I want to get on with my course. You know how important it is to me."

"I won't get in your way."

She sighs. "It's not just that."

"It's him, ain't it?"

"Look Russell and I … it's not what you think."

"So what's the problem?"

"You. Drugs. You're still taking them, aren't you?"

"Not much."

She shakes her head. "That means you are. God, that's what I hate most of all."

"What?"

"The way you think about *them* all the time. Not even another woman but something inanimate."

"I'll give them up tomorrow if you come back."

"The thing is," she says, opening the van door. "I can't trust you any more, Michael. You lied about the needles and I've already risked too much going with you." Then she leans across and gives him a peck on the cheek. "Look, I'm going to my mum's for Christmas. You can give me a ring there if you like and we can have a chat."

But when he phones there on Boxing Day, the only person doing the chatting is her mother. Sorry Michael, she says, but Catrina's not well at the moment. Oh nothing serious, probably just too many glasses of sherry and mince pies, you know how it is. Why don't you call back in a day or so? She should have perked up by then.

But she hasn't. On New Year's Eve, her mother tells him that Catrina's still poorly and it wasn't the rich food, after all, but some kind of bug that seems to have knocked her for six, and why don't you try again in a few days?

By the second week of January, he's onto something. He finally gets to speak to Catrina, but she isn't in any hurry to get back to college. Something must have happened. Something serious. It must be if she's lost all interest in her course.

"Are you sitting down?" she says.

It's bad news, he knew it. ME or cancer or maybe he's infected her with HIV and now she's slowly dying …

"You may as well know. You're going to find out sooner or later. " She sighs. "Michael, I'm pregnant… and before you go jumping to any conclusions, it isn't yours."

They both know whose it is, she goes on, although she won't actually say the name Russell. Just 'he' and 'his' and how 'he' doesn't want to know because 'he' says 'he's' too young for such a responsibility and she can understand that. "Of course, it was an accident but I've decided to have it anyway – here at my mum's."

It seems to Michael that she's got it all worked out. She's been in touch with her tutor, she explains, who will defer her place until next January if she wants. She doesn't even have to pack in college at all, seeing as it's not due until half way through August but she feels lousy and she can't be doing with all the gossip from those students who are still incredibly immature, and suddenly he no longer resents Russell or Russell's baby: he's simply happy knowing that 'he' is off the scene at last; that Catrina's now safe from all those influences and distractions and temptations.

*

Michael regards Catrina's mother as an honest, decent sort. Okay, she lied about Catrina having the flu but she had her arm twisted; she did it for her daughter. But when he phoned just a few moments ago she said, "I'm afraid Catrina's out at the moment, Michael, but actually I'm glad you've phoned." Before he had time to wonder what gladdened her she went on, "I know I shouldn't be saying this but I think you ought to have this information anyway. It's about Catrina's dates. The baby's due in early July, not mid-August. Do you understand what I'm trying to tell you?"

But when he goes to see Catrina in person to tackle her about it she's brusque with him. Brusque and defensive. "So? It's due in July. What of it?"

"You told me it was August."

"July, August, what difference does it make?"

"Paternal rights, that's what."

"Okay, I'll tell you why I said August. Because I didn't want you getting any ideas it was yours."

"But it could be mine if it's due in July."

She raises her hands definitively. "No way. We weren't sleeping together after I started college. We were more like brother and sister by then so don't try and make me look a tart. All those drugs may have fucked up your memory but mine's fine, thank you very much. "

He can't pinpoint exact dates and times, it's true; he doesn't have her needle-sharp memory, making it easy for her to browbeat him.

"I don't care if it ain't mine," he says with sudden decisiveness. "I still want to see you. I'll help you look after it and everything."

She shakes her head. "It won't work. I need to be on my own. Just me and the baby when it comes, and my mum."

*

The next time Michael's on the phone, Catrina's mother puts her case more forcefully. "I know I shouldn't be saying this because Catrina told me in confidence who the father was and made me promise not to tell you because she didn't want her child brought up by a drug addict. Her words, not mine. But I told her you've got a right to know if it's your child." She lets out a big sigh, like a great weight's shifted. "I said to her, if you don't tell him then I will, because I can't carry on lying on your behalf. I told her it's not fair on me and it's not fair on you, Michael. Of course, she'll go mad when she finds out. But you've got to do what you think's right, haven't you?"

So now Catrina's mum looks upon him as a son. She invites him over for hot meals and a warm bed because she reckons it must get really cold in that camper van at night, and by March he's spending every other weekend in Newbury. Long weekends sleeping, or pretending to sleep while overhearing conversations or arguments. Catrina doesn't want him there whereas her mum does. Her mum wants them to be together, as a couple, like before – if only for the sake of what's in the best interests of her grandchild. Surely the child would be better off with some family stability? Won't Catrina give Michael another chance, for the sake of the baby?

"It's the baby I'm thinking of, mum. It won't have a stable life with a father on drugs."

"But you and Michael used to be like love's young dream– "

"Don't start on that again because I'm not in the mood."

"A pair of young hippies travelling around in their battered old van without a care in the world…"

"I used to think he was a hippy but he's not. He hasn't got that laid-back optimism. He's nihilistic and self-destructive." The kitchen cupboards are shut with decisive bangs. "It's not what I'm about. My philosophy on life is wholesome. OK, I've done a bit of organic stuff, but needles are a whole different ball game." Her voice takes on a different tone. "It really made my stomach churn, the way he got off on a needle, the way he strangled his arm with a tourniquet. He doesn't know I saw him but I did, through the keyhole when we were living together, and it just looked so barbaric and warped, a bit like someone about to hang himself and that's when I knew we were– "

"Keep your voice down, he might hear you."

"I don't care. Let him hear. I'm sick of my life being restricted in this way. It wasn't my idea to let him stay here. I can't even go into the sitting-room because he's crashed out on the settee half the time."

"But he was so tired when he arrived this afternoon and he doesn't look as if he'd had a square meal since he was last here."

"And whose fault's that? It just goes to show he's totally incapable of looking after a child. He can't even look after himself. "

Catrina's mother tells her not to be too hard on him and even goes to get a blanket from the bottom of her wardrobe to spread across his half-asleep body while she's talking.

"You know you're trouble, mum. You're too soft."

6

As soon as she puts her key in the front door, Cheryl feels a presence – someone waiting for her inside. There she is. Sitting in Mrs Howard's lounge-cum-waiting-room in a long fisherman's jumper and black lycra leggings, clutching twenty Marlborough. She looks skinny as a thread, premature lines around the mouth, and wearing little make-up.

It's been well over eighteen months. After many false alarms, they finally left the flatlet across the landing for good – Elaine and Matt – and Cheryl's not heard a dicky bird since, until now. But how did Elaine get in, anyway? It must have been Mrs Howard. Well-meaning, sees-good-in-everyone Mrs Howard.

"I wish you'd phone before coming," Cheryl says, as Elaine follows her upstairs.

Elaine curls her lip. "Phones. The very death of spontaneity."

"I'm surprised you didn't bring Matt."

"That nerd. I dumped him years ago. I'm with Horse now."

"Horse? What sort of a name is that?"

"What about you then, mum? Not found yourself another bloke yet?"

"Me? I'm far too busy these days."

"You never are." Elaine roots about in the fridge until she finds something she fancies. Some fruit flan. "Have you spoken to dad in the last few months at all?"

"No. Why, have you?"

"Not for a few months. He hadn't heard any more from Michael, when I last spoke."

Cheryl stops in her tracks. "What do you mean, any more?"

In order to carry on, she's had to shove all that stuff away in a corner, that stuff Michael said about Andrew and the abuse, shoved it away in a dark cellar of her mind, out of the way. She can't face dealing with it. Not at the moment. Maybe never. But any other information about her missing son is seized upon.

"Didn't you know?" Elaine is saying. "They met up...so did I."

"*You*? When?"

"I dunno, ages ago now."

"Come on, think. How long ago?"

"Over a year, I suppose. Michael worked with dad for a while too, before doing his usual disappearing act."

"So you've all been ganging up on me – keeping it a secret, eh?" Elaine shrugs.

"So what's Michael like now? Where's he living then?"

"I dunno. Southampton, last I heard. Why do you pretend to care, anyway?"

"Oh don't be like that, Elaine," she says, trying her best to endear herself to her daughter.

"And it's Lainie, for your information," Elaine says with a scowl. "It has been for ages."

*

The following day, Elaine drops another bombshell. "I'm not going back to Bournemouth," she says. "I spoke to Mrs Howard this morning about flats, and she said I could rent my old room again. No point in leaving it empty she said."

And so, as before, Elaine moves in to the flat across the way and disappears back to Bournemouth regularly – returning each time with a different point of view.

– I don't want to lead your carcinogenic lifestyle.

– I hate this throw-away society.

– It's shit, this hole-in-the-wall mentality.

She'll say such things out of the blue. Unprovoked. Cheryl finds there's nothing in Elaine she can warm to, and probably vice versa. Maybe they're too alike. Then there's all that business with the mirrors. It's not as if it's pleasure or vanity, holding Elaine there in a distorted gaze for hours on end, it's obsession. She wants to be doing something else, somewhere else: some lost or yet-to-be discovered hobby maybe, but first of all, before that, she needs to be satisfied with herself, her bodily self. She can't seem to get past the skin. Certainly she wants constant reassurance that she looks okay. Always that – do I look okay? Cheryl understands it up to a point, she felt the same at her age. But Elaine's so tyrannical in the way she asks it, Cheryl no longer feels she has a choice of reply. Because the truth is Elaine doesn't look okay. She looks in a bad way. She's got spots that won't heal and a look in her eyes that no longer sees behind, to the person, to the meaning expressed, but has shifted to the front, to the surface, to the skin, to shallow things like lines and blemishes. Mum, do you put anything on your crow's-feet? How do you get rid of orange-peel skin, mum? And Cheryl feels it rubbing off on her, making her mourn the loss of her own youth and glamour.

Not only this, but Elaine's days are all topsy-turvy. She sleeps at odd times and Cheryl doesn't like to disturb her, because it's only when Elaine's asleep that she doesn't have that fraught look or that ugly short fuse. But awake, Elaine is like a crabby old woman – cynical about the world and faddy about her diet which is a peculiar marriage of the most healthy and the most junky: mung beans and coke, kombu and pizza.

If it's sunny, Elaine will occasionally venture out into the back garden to sit on the low wall and smoke, always in black, as if trying to absorb all the heat into her until, fed up, she shuffles back indoors, hating the summer. Sometimes, at nine o'clock in the evening or later, she'll want to go out to the shops and Cheryl will go with her, thinking that it's a takeaway or off-license that she wants. No, Elaine will say. I just wanted to look at the shop-windows, now they're all closed and lit-up. Most of the time though, she doesn't have the desire to go anywhere. Most of the time she's atrophied and her sense of youth deserted her. She doesn't say anything much of substance and even the elusive Horse, on the rare occasions he phones and asks to speak to Lainie, is told to Fuck Off.

7

Faith is sitting in the office, holding the fort, when there's a knock on the door. On her desk, her tea has been standing around too long and there's a list of phone calls she's yet to return. Typical that it should get this busy with Anthea away at a conference, Jeff over at the Willows, Cheryl out taking one of the residents to the doctor's, and Peggy – well Peggy is just Peggy: renowned for looking industrious, though actually achieving very little of practical worth. Thankfully, there are the other volunteers who have their wits about them.

Faith opens the door.

"Michael!" she says. "Well, look at you!"

At his side is a young woman with a pram.

"This is Catrina," he says.

His physical appearance looks similar, though he's put on a few pounds, but there's something different about him. He's more or less drug-free maybe. Or it's the way he holds his head or looks her in the eye when he speaks.

"And this is Shea."

"Oh my!" she says, unsure of the baby's gender. "Can Auntie Faith have a hold?"

She notices how Catrina seems very much in the forefront when it comes to the baby. "Your nails are dirty, Michael," she says, as he hovers over the pram.

"Well," says Catrina, returning the baby to its pram, once Faith has had a chance to make a big fuss. "I'll let you two talk on your own for a bit while I take Shea for a walk."

"So," says Faith, when Catrina closes the door behind her. "Tell me all your news."

"Well, I went to college in the end. You know, after you brought those leaflets over. I chickened out of my exams, mind. But if I hadn't have gone to college I'd never have met Catrina and had Shea."

He tells her all about being on the road last summer. She can well imagine. She can imagine the Dick Whittington bundle and the cow-pats and the Glastonbury socks. But how nice to have done all the festivals, year upon year. How nice, when you're older, to hang up your hat, at last, and live on your memories and tales of your adventures. This, she thinks, must be why Social Security ministers, and the like, are bent on driving these people off the road and out of existence. They're envious really, and she is too. Travellers give her itchy feet and a primitive longing for a nomadic life around bonfires. Michael's generation is nomadic by nature, whether traveller on the road or yuppie on the social climb. Only the older generation is static. The middle generation, hers, is pulled both ways.

She subdues her expression, suddenly remembering something else. "Did you ever track down your father?"

"Yeah," he says, and tells her all about the phone boxes and the Tooting house and Waterloo station. "But he doesn't know about Shea. I don't want my folks to have any part of him. I've achieved him all on my own."

He gazes through the window. "At first I was hoping Shea would be a girl...it would have been easier, you know?"

"Easier?"

"I get this block sometimes and then I can't hold him. I'm afraid to. Afraid I might hurt him."

"But you've turned a corner, Michael."

"I do love him, don't get me wrong. It's just, self-destruction's part of my nature and I might destroy him because he's a part of me, ain't he?"

"But you've got insight. You're airing your fears and that's good. You know I'm always here if you need to talk to someone. "

"Cheers."

And suddenly she can picture him in two, three, five years time as this superdad, loving Shea to bits, and with a new spiritual depth. An achiever – feverishly accomplishing things to prove a point, to himself more than anyone, making a name for himself, swiftly, from nowhere, possibly heralding a radical new approach in the treatment of drug addiction, an alternative therapy perhaps, and running experiential workshops to people who may well wonder just where such awareness and compassion and humanity could have come from ...

8

Cheryl returns to Chrysalis with the resident she accompanied to the doctor's and finds a blond girl sitting in the empty coffee lounge. At first she thinks the girl is alone, but then she sees she's holding something. A baby. A tiny baby, at that.

"Hello," Cheryl says, imagining the girl to be an applicant for the Willows. But there haven't been such little babies in the Willows yet, only bigger children. "Can I help?"

"I'm just waiting for my boyfriend," says the girl.

Cheryl sits down and smiles at the little baby who looks just like Michael did at that age. "A boy?"

"Yes."

"What's his name?"

"Shea."

"Do you mind if I– ?"

"Not at all," says the girl as she hands over the baby to Cheryl and there's something about that milky fragrance, that faint tang of poo, those fidgety little fingers still forming a grasp, still working out how it's done, which awakens an old feeling. Not a pain exactly, but something visceral. Appetite. Craving. An itch in the womb.

Faith once remarked – Faith the 'recovering' addict, who hasn't touched an opiate in years – that even to this day, even after years of abstinence, she still has cravings for the opiate drugs and if she sees some tin foil or half a lemon, it can still make her go all peculiar. But this is worse than the lemon or the foil, this is the thing itself, like if someone were to smoke heroin in front of Faith.

Cheryl quickly hands the baby back to its mother and hurries outside for some air.

Through the window, she just catches sight of some of the residents as they trickle into the coffee lounge and gather round the baby. She remembers it so well: the popularity, the adoring words coming at you like gifts. Isn't he sweet? You must be so proud. Isn't he just like you?

She gets back in her car and races home. She can't possibly work this afternoon. In fact, she needs a few days off.

Back home, she still feels sick and dizzy. She peels herself an orange and holds a sticky segment up to the window. There it is. The little pip now visible through the translucent wall. We are one but two. It was Diana, she passed it all on. But it's too late to take down the boards and open up her room, just one more time. She's nearly forty-eight.

Across the landing, she sees Elaine's door open and bursts in.

"We've run out of eggs," says Elaine, not looking up from her VIZ.

What made her say that? About running out of eggs?

"I want another baby, Elaine."

"Don't talk stupid. You're too old."

"Perhaps if you had one then."

"I've got one. He's called Horse."

"I mean, you could have a real baby. For me."

"Oh I don't want one of those. Not ever."

"You say that now."

"Having babies is dangerous and self-indulgent. The world's bursting at the seams as it is."

"I used to think like you."

"I mean, who's it all for anyway – this having babies shit? No one wants them once they're big – these babies of yesterday."

"You're very cynical for someone so young."

"Before having babies people should try and imagine their little darlings as old people with no teeth and dementia and pacemakers and Zimmer frames. They'd soon think twice about having them then, I bet."

"What are you going on about? And where are you going dressed like that? I can virtually see your knickers."

"So? You've totally ruined my enjoyment of Fat Slags, so I'm off out."

9

Cheryl clip-clops down the high street in her smart shoes and red double-breasted suit with buttons that gleam, feeling omnipotent, her hair in the tightest bun with its blond highlights. She's on her way to the two day Addiction Awareness course, being held right here in Winchester, as luck would have it. It makes a refreshing change to get out and about sometimes, because Chrysalis is in one of its humdrum cycles again. There's just nothing to bite into with these Heroin Housewives, such ordinary people, so widespread is the problem these days. But they still get all that counselling. What a luxury to be the listened to. What exquisite self-indulgence.

She looks at her watch and, having located the right building, hurries to the suite where the first session is being held. Most of the other course participants – substance misuse workers they call themselves nowadays – are already seated and, look, there's old Peggy grinning away sycophantically at some self-important person. Peggy, who's never ceased to amaze her, simply because she's survived a staggering length of time at Chrysalis, in spite of her fundamental ineptitude. But she can't escape Peggy now, not for this first session, anyway, because Peggy's frantically patting the empty chair beside her – the one she's saved specially for Cheryl. Even when the larger group splits off into smaller groups of five or six to discuss the meaning of addiction and to examine personal attitudes, Peggy is still there.

Their group, Group Two, are discussing their own addictions – tea, coffee, bars of chocolate, you name it – and now Peggy is about to widen the debate. She used to be addicted to the sun, she says. She simply had to go out in it. "I was going to say come rain or shine," Peggy says and everyone laughs. She's endeared herself to them already. Anyway, she would get extremely agitated if she had to sit indoors, she tells Group Two. She simply had to keep up that tan. If it faded, well, she just had to get another dose. Dose. You see? The same language, says Peggy. Half the time her tan hadn't faded at all, but it stopped being a rational thing. If there were weeks of cloudy weather, she got depressed. The sun seems to have properties that make people feel better, says Peggy, and if she got a good dose she felt merry, she felt sun-drunk, she felt confident. She and lots of others. Fortunately, she never had enough to cause sunstroke or skin cancer (fingers crossed), or other sun-related diseases, but there are others who don't heed the dangers, and what Peggy is saying suddenly seems pregnant with wisdom, Cheryl thinks, remembering for an instant that woozy hot summer when she first met Luigi. She seems to have underestimated Peggy, who clearly has hidden talents.

*

Babies, Cheryl thinks as she clip clops home after Day One of the conference, swinging her briefcase and braving the December elements, because home is only a ten minute walk. People were coming out with all sorts – work, relationships, golf, knitting. But babies? That's a bit kooky, isn't it? There, she's said it. The words have taken shape behind her lips. She was addicted to the feeling that babies give. Elaine was her first hit, never to be repeated because you never can, and Juliet was the new, dark, seductive drug, her crack cocaine if you like, the child of a romantic encounter, always a bit different from the crowd, and then she kicked it all, she tried to terminate that feeling because she never wanted to be mumsy, or to lose her sense of self in her children, not completely, not at all. She always preferred singing to having kids, truth be told. But maybe that's it. Maybe that's what your children come to despise ultimately. Maybe that's why hers have demonized her. Michael most of all.

But tomorrow she will see him, at last. It's printed there in black and white on the programme inside her briefcase. It says, Talk from Service Users: Two Users Share their Experience of Overcoming their Addiction. He will be one of them, she knows that for certain, because Faith confirmed it. She's got to hand it to him. It will take some guts to stand up in front of all these people, and she will be sitting at the back of the conference hall in the dimmed light, her heart pounding, until the afternoon coffee break when she will snake through everyone, tap him on the arm and say –

But hullo? What's that police car doing outside Mrs Howard's house, and who's that scantily-clad red-head climbing into it? Didn't she just toss a mobile phone into that hedge, and hang on, that looks like Elaine talking to that police woman and why's she dressed in that thin gauzy thing with half her back showing on an icy afternoon like this? And she's getting into the police car too, but excuse me that's my daughter you've got in there. Where are you taking her? What do you mean, under arrest? Possession of a Class A drug? You must have made a mistake. Elaine's not into drugs. What happened,

Elaine? Don't worry, I'll follow you down to the station.

But what's happened, Elaine? I can hardly start the bloody car for shaking and this is a fine time to be thinking about a never-ending egg within egg and Russian dolls and sowing the divine seed from age to age, but it all went completely down the tubes. That's how it starts every time, in fact – with the tubes. The Fallopian sort, but I hate these dark winter afternoons, when you can't see ahead, you never can when you're on the tail of a dirty great lorry but I'm right behind you, and anyway, Elaine, whatever happened to that magic pink light? When did it go? Was it when toothbrushes stopped having curly hair? But I expect they'll only caution you as it's a first offence and then can we start afresh? All of us?

But what happens to us, Elaine? And tell me, what colour is Wednesday?

###

If you have enjoyed this story, you might consider writing a review on Amazon or any other site. Reviews not only help other readers enjoy the books you have but also help the author. They can also help you build your reputation as a reviewer.

About the author:

Kate Rigby was born in Crosby, Liverpool and now lives in Devon. She's been writing novels for over forty years. She loves cats, singing, music, photography and LFC. She is also an armchair campaigner.

Discover other titles by Kate Rigby by visiting:

http://kjrbooks.yolasite.com/

Or her occasional blogs:

http://bubbitybooks.blogspot.co.uk/

Printed in Great Britain
by Amazon

21359920R00092